→ THE ←
BITTER HALF

THE
BITTER HALF
TOBY OLSON

FC2

TUSCALOOSA

The University of Alabama Press
Tuscaloosa, Alabama 35487-0380

Published by FC2, an imprint of the University of Alabama Press, with support provided by Florida State University and the Publications Unit of the
Department of English at Illinois State University

Address all editorial inquiries to: Fiction Collective Two, Florida State
University, c/o English Department, Tallahassee, FL 32306-1580

⊗

Library of Congress Cataloging-in-Publication Data
Olson, Toby
  The bitter half / Toby Olson.— 1st ed.
    p. cm.
  "Fiction Collective Two"
  ISBN-13: 978-1-57366-132-4 (pbk. : alk. paper)
  ISBN-10: 1-57366-132-5 (pbk. : alk. paper)
  I. Title.
  PS3565.L84B54 2006
  813'.54—dc22

                      2006007001

Cover Design: Lou Robinson
Book Design: Erin Guimon and Tara Reeser
Typeface: Baskerville
Produced and printed in the United States of America

✦✦

Always, for Miriam

✦✦

Parts of this novel appeared in
Washington Square and *The New Review*,
and two chapters were published
as a limited edition book called *Depression Dog*
by The Perishable Press Limited in 2003.

pollard 1. A tree whose top branches have been cut back to the trunk so that it may produce a dense growth of new shoots. 2. An animal, such as an ox, a goat, or a sheep, that no longer has its horns.

—*The American Heritage Dictionary*

✈ONE✦

I met him when I was consulting at a prison outside of Pearce in the southeast corner of Arizona. He was boyish still at twenty-one, yet known as a wily criminal, and they had fixed up a good place for him and were concerned only with the Mexicans.

Pearce is no more than forty miles from the Mexican border, and the desert gives way to foothills and shade south of Tombstone in about eight. And breaking out was relatively easy, given good fellowship and the dull desperations of their approach. It was patchwork; they'd fix the leak, then others would spring up.

Most of the Mexicans were taken on dusty streets and in bars in the border towns, Naco and Agua Prieta, sometimes as far west as Nogales. They must have felt some safety in their home country after the long trek, unaware of agreements at the local level, a few dollars to informers near the crossing. The prison would send down men to get them, Chicanos for the most part, but there were those who had wits enough to continue south, beyond Cananea, and were lost to them forever. It was 'thirty-five and so was I, a child of the troubled century, and it was these prison breaks they'd brought me there to deal with.

The sky was overcast, but I wore a plantation hat, as much for the look of it as for the filtered sun. They'd given me a dozen prisoners to dig test holes at measured distances along the fenced perimeter. This was always the first thing and was often perfunctory, and I found myself gazing out over the desert and the purple sage, those worn down foothills in the distance quite distinct and beautiful under the cloudy sky. Mexico was a real promise at the end of that vision, a constant urging, and I was wondering about the advisability of a canvas screening sewn to the fence in order to block that view.

They'd sent the architectural renderings ahead, but no blueprints, and in the letter an obvious hint that this was political money, what little was around those days, public relations for those seeking office on the back of the Great Depression. It was clear they'd hired me only to cover their own simple incompetence.

The renderings presented a blatantly obvious plan, nothing of interest and no possibility of surprises, and though I had no need of work or of the money—my father's will had provided amply for the latter—I'd taken the job because I had a little free time and had never been in that part of the country.

"Maybe I can fly," he'd said.

A brim helps a hat form a secret window between cheekbones and brow, an isolating rectangle, and in the shade of mine I felt dramatic and disguised as I turned to that voice and saw him pressed against the wire, his fingers curled in the links at his shoulders. He had short blond hair, a cowlick at his brow, and I could see the terms of a squalid world beyond him.

They'd dragged a metal shed from somewhere, the size of an outhouse. It even had a vented chimney in its flat roof. It was elevated on cinder blocks, and there was a view between them to the back wall of his wire cage. The shed was visible from all sides. It had a small window covered in wire mesh above its door. He had privacy, but it would be hot in there, even under cloud cover. A bucket sat a few feet away for shitting; he could piss in the hot sand at the perimeter, take his meals on the brief wooden steps. The cage was open to the sky, and I saw him glance up there. Then he lowered his head and smiled at me. It's nothing at all, his look said, a piece of cake. He could leave when he wanted to.

"Pollard!"

The guard escorted me to the warden's office, a cramped room with a fan blowing over a block of ice at the window. He had his feet up on the desk, a beefy little man, and he glanced to the brim of my plantation hat and smirked when I told him my thoughts about the canvas vision screen.

"Check the résumé," I said.

"I have, I have. But that's all in the East, and you don't know Mexicans."

I doubted that. I'd had enough dealings over the years to know about men and their nature.

"You understand," he said, "this is a boondoggle. It's political. So long as we go through the paces and I get your report."

"And the kid in the cage," I said. "What about him?"

"You're not here for that. It's the Mexicans and those assholes over the border, it's *their* concern. That we're letting criminals loose to go back in again, what with the economic situation. It's the politicians, on both sides. So long as we go through the paces."

I knew the kid had his ways. He'd been in five different prisons since nineteen-thirty when he was first taken. He'd escaped from all of them. And I could tell, too, that what they had going for him here was seriously flawed. They thought if they could only see him, guards and lights, they'd have him. But he had his privacy within that little shed.

I still wore my hat and he hadn't offered me a seat. I kept my mouth shut about that.

"I've got about a week," I said. "The cells, mess hall, and the infirmary. The yard and perimeter fencing seem okay. I'll have to check the work schedules, the entertainments."

"There aren't any."

It was Wednesday. "By next Thursday," I said. "I'll have it written up."

I worked through the weekend. The clouds left and the heat came on again, ferociously, and I drove into Tombstone on Saturday to get some lighter clothing. I found a broad umbrella there as well and used it against the sun when I was studying things on the outside, beyond the fence where they put the prisoners to work clearing desert brush. The guards hid their smiles, but the Mexicans seemed appreciative of my ingenuity.

I examined the cells carefully. There was nothing in the mess hall or infirmary. The well and septic tank were inside the perimeter, and though the yard was porous sand, the fence was set in concrete, a wall that went down more than twenty feet into the ground. And they weren't going over the fence or through it either.

The place was sound as it could be, and I think I knew early on that the matter was purely cultural. They were in it together, Chicanos, Mexicans, and the few gringos there, all two hundred of them. I knew it in their faces in the exercise yard and from the words I'd passed with a few of them in my peregrinations.

I wrote it up, made prominent reference to the vision-fence to put my mark on it, and even suggested a variation on the mirrors I'd used to great effect in Nova Scotia.

In that case, the prison sat on a high promontory at the edge of sea, and the mirrors had aided the tower guards in finding escapees as they moved down through the rocky declivities that were ripe with hiding places. They also presented the wayward with their own desperate images, surprising there and disorienting. Here they could set the mirrors out in the desert on the back side, where the lights of Pearce were a promise. These were not complex changes, though beyond their dull imaginings after all, and I knew that nothing I could suggest would come to anything.

I wrote then the more significant answer to their problems, that they had a community, ready-made, and needed to turn its energies inward. Sports and recreation, a few books in a library, better food. This would keep the short timers there and get the others to think twice about the matter. I ended my report with a few more specifics about the physical plant, but they were of little consequence.

It was Thursday morning when I finished, and after I'd filed the carbon and packed my suitcases, I dressed in the white linen suit and drove out to the prison from Pearce. The warden wasn't there, but the kid was, and once I'd delivered the manila envelope and was heading back across the yard, I saw him urinating off in a corner of his cage and caught his eye as he smiled over his shoulder.

I had a Monday train reservation out of Tucson and the whole weekend ahead of me. My next job was a fortnight away, a chain gang prison in bayou country down in Louisiana, issues of suicide and ineffective brutality. I'd arrive back in Wisconsin by the end of the week, would have a few cool days at the cabin before I set out again.

It was incredibly hot, and once I'd slipped off the white jacket and reached in to crank open the Ford's windshield, I braved the heat of the car's oven, heading south on the dusty road toward Tombstone and the promise of those cooling foothills.

Tombstone offered little, though I found a room at the edge of town with a fan at the window and in moments felt the sweat drying away in the cool breeze riding down from the San Pedro mountains. The town was sleepy in the summer heat, waiting for the tourists that were not coming. There was the Birdcage Theater, the Tombstone Epitaph, and the OK Corral, but the weight of Depression sat heavily here, as through the entire country. Doors were locked up tight, windows rendered opaque by desert dust.

I sat under fans at the Crystal Palace, sipping a beer. I'd changed into flannel pants, almost pajama-like, and a gaucho shirt I'd purchased in Argentina a few years before. Warmer clothes were laid out for the next day's journey, when I'd be heading for the mountains and the town of Bisbee. There were a few cowboys drinking in the Palace. They watched me suspiciously, at least until I called for beers around, wiping my brow dramatically with my handkerchief.

The next morning brought a light, soothing rain, and I was happy for the umbrella I'd purchased earlier as I loaded my suitcases into the Ford's trunk. People stood in the streets, looking up in wonderment as I passed them. The clouds were moving swiftly, and I could see the place where sun brightened the sage-brush beyond a veil of mist. It was raining, and it was deep into the summer. Then the rain was gone.

Bisbee was more interesting than Tombstone. An open-pit copper mining town, it nestled in the mountains a few thousand feet above the desert plain. The pit itself was in operation, albeit with a skeleton crew, and was billed as the largest in the U.S. It was truly impressive, testing the terms of distance vision, a whole world of weather and activity between one side and the other. Still, it was a hole in the ground, and I quit my examinations early, shopped the main street for a while, then returned to the hotel and read. I was tired after the week's work, and rather than venturing out again, I ate lightly in the hotel diner, then retired early and slept late into the morning of the next day.

At one I put in a call to Danker.

"It's two o'clock here," he said. He always said the time when I checked in.

"Any mail? Phone calls?"

"Just a few weary travelers, looking for work. I put them on to clearing brush, pulling weeds in the maze. Avery Brattle called."

"*Again?*" I said.

He laughed. "Doesn't seem to get the point, I guess."

"It's been hot as hell here," I said.

"Not here. They wrote from Louisiana to confirm. I sent them your arrival time. There's no other mail to speak of."

"What about Southpaw and Bret, what's up with them?"

"They're okay, just fine. They brought the girls over yesterday. The upper rooms are aired, and they took care of your father's study and the kitchen. They'll be back for the rest of the downstairs in a day or two. The girls I mean. Bret's working at the cabin."

"Sounds good," I said. "Did Avery have anything at all to say?"

"No. Nothing. He wants to see you though."

"I'm sure he does."

"I told him I didn't know your exact schedule. Are you coming back soon?"

"Middle of the week," I said. "Thursday at the latest. It depends on the Union Pacific."

"Keep cool," he said.

I read for most of the day, a book about penal institutions and the social end of things. Such issues had arisen in my work dramatically in recent consultations, and though my interest was in physical plants exclusively, solutions often came in other terms, softer and more ambiguous ones, and now I was thinking ahead to that Louisiana deal and what might be at issue there.

I was taking notes when I noticed the paper darkening, and when I looked at my watch I saw it was already seven-thirty. If I was going to head down into Mexico, I'd better get started. I wore a blue chambray shirt and a pair of jeans and took the straw hat along. I had deck shoes, but I put the work boots on instead. I knew I couldn't be inconspicuous, but I could at least avoid a tourist look. I wanted to see the place where the Pearce prison Mexicans escaped to, if only to put some flesh on the end of things and get the recent consultation behind me.

Naco, black chewing tobacco; that was the name of the town and its translation, a typical dusty border town where they hosed the dirt streets with water and hosed the few gringos they could get their hands on. There'd be no law in the place, except for money, and little of that, and I left my watch and rings and even the diamond stud in the hotel safe before heading out. The town was only a few miles away, but down below the foothills, and when I stopped at the border crossing I could feel the heat in the stone kiosk as I leaned out.

Beyond the border, there was very little to be seen in the darkness. I passed down a street with a few shops on the left, all locked up for the night, then turned at an unmarked corner and came in sight of the only activity about.

Bar lights bathed the edges of the dirt square, two active *tabernas* and a quieter one all in a row. I could hear music coming from open doorways well before I got there. Four trucks and a half-dozen rusted out cars were parked awkwardly below the boardwalk, and beyond were the shadow figures of low, ramshackle houses along side streets, a few dim bulbs behind cloth-covered windows.

Three women were passing out through the door of the Casa Rojo as I pulled in. Heels and thick makeup. Fifty-cent whores, they laughed and poked each other when they saw me. I waved them off as I climbed the steps, then headed for the Blue Moon, the quieter place at the end.

It was dark inside and almost empty. The bartender sat on a high stool at the bar's end, talking quietly to an old man in bib overalls and a baseball cap. The only other customers were four silent cowboys, elbows at the rail, their Stetsons hiding their heads entirely. There was a jukebox off in a corner and a few small tables. Above the bottles behind the bar, the wall was hung with crooked pictures, views of the town in better days, I thought, though I could barely make out the images.

I moved to the bar's end and called softly for *cerveza*. When I heard the scraping of the bartender's stool, I noticed the sound was coming from the wrong place, not there, but over my right shoulder. I turned to a dim, yellow light, the edge of a shit-stained toilet bowl as the door down the hallway opened, then saw his head come up as he touched the walls to get his bearings. I saw the cowlick then, and under it his smile of recognition.

→TWO←

"No more than a month this time," he said.

I'd bought beer and we'd moved to a table near the wall. One of the cowboys dropped some *pesos*, but the jukebox volume was set low and the mournful love strains only gave us privacy in our conversation. He was shaky after his journey. Still, he continued to be elated in the flush of his escape.

"We're a little ironic," I said.

"You mean it's your job to keep us in, and mine's to get out?"

He'd been at the Pearce prison for a year and had escaped twice before they put him in the cage. Upon his arrival, he'd been a celebrity, and his escapes had given both heart and permission to many others. This was the big one though. They'd be leaking out of there at a good pace from now on.

"The best one?"

"No. Not that. The chain gang in Louisiana was much better. They beat us into exhaustion there, people killed themselves. The place was fortified like a castle. This was a piece of cake."

"I'll be going there."

"To Louisiana? Really? It's all brutality. It can work for a while to cover up the flaws, but even *they* had to back off at times."

"You know," I said, "this is the wrong place to be. They'll be looking here."

"Of course," he said. "That's what I want. To go back and see their faces, especially the warden."

"What about freedom? Don't you want that?"

"What for?" he said. "This is what I do."

I ordered frijoles and a plate of corn tortillas, more beer and two shots of tequila which the bartender delivered to our table in water glasses. There was a kitchen back behind the bar somewhere, and we could smell the burn of oil, the rich darkness of the beans. The napkins were rough, only a small rectangle beside each fork, so I pushed mine over to him and opened the large cotton handkerchief to spread across my knees.

He ate slowly and delicately, savoring every mouthful, touching the napkins to the edges of his lips. They were thin lips, though expressive, and he looked into my eyes and smiled often. He seemed sophisticated and yet at the same time childlike, especially when he spoke about the dog.

"Old Buck," he said, and I could see the moisture of vivid memory in his eyes.

He spoke of his early years, near Omaha, after his father died. He'd been raised up as a farm boy there. "I was sixteen years old. Buck was a hunter, active in the snow even, and a good retriever."

And in the summers they would go for rabbit, sometimes, in the fall, pheasant. He had the broad head of a bull and was as high as the kid's waist at the shoulder, and he was three years old at that time, frisky and still adolescent, enthusiastic about the hunt and the play too. He was fast and very strong, but gentle. He loved children, but then he'd downed and taken the kid's sister away, that sweet little girl.

The kid was out in the barn, searching among the peaches his mother had stored in the dark there in a basket, snapping the weevils between thumbnail and finger. Each one was the man's will, his stepfather raging in drunkenness, disposed of with a careless flick. He had no use for him, but he was not big enough yet, and the touch of the tender fruit brought up his mother, his little sister, and what might be the responsibility he could not earn.

It was late summer, a Friday after the harvest. They were out there in their places on the sloping lawn that ended where the woods started, and he could see the undulations in the humid swarms of insects up at the tree tops through the large rectangle of light at the barn door, and could see his sister too.

She was sitting in the grass on the quilt his mother had sewn for her before his father's death, down on the lawn below where they would be, his mother taking the clothes down and ironing and his stepfather, Mr. Jones, drinking as he had for the entire week. Buck saw the kid looking and whined softly, pushing his muzzle against the boy's leg where he sat on the low, three-legged stool beside the peaches. His sister was playing, toying with objects on the quilt. Her dress was clear up to her thighs, and he could see the dark marks at her knobby knees and along her little bowed legs. Only two years old, and he'd just turned sixteen.

He heard the man cough and spit, some guarded warbling from his mother, high-pitched and constricted, then the slap of a shirt or sheet as she pulled the pins away. It might have been his father there beside her and not Mr. Jones, the name he insisted upon to teach them proper manners, but there was no use at all in such imagining, nor in his dull, abstracted aloneness since his mother had remarried. For him she'd said, and for his sister, and for the farm too. Buck rose at his side, and they both moved into the door's light, but into a stripe of shadow at the barn side, where he sat and Buck squatted on his haunches, his tail tapping at the barn's boards and he leaning back in the shade against them. Now he could see them.

His mother was working the iron over the board, a shirt sleeve waving down like a windsock at its edge. She wore a bonnet acting as blinders, though it was hazy and the sun was dull, and she had to turn her head to see Mr. Jones. Behind her the house was large, opulent even in its disrepair, thick tapered columns at the broad porch edges and above them two stories and the four graceful bays under the eaves. *Her* house, he thought, but it made no difference, though even the clothesline Mr. Jones had bolted to a corner column didn't quite sully it. That line went down the sloping lawn to a high, anchored pole, and another pole tented the clothes hanging from it, sheets, pillowcases, and the man's shirts, trousers, and yellowed underwear, all dancing in a gentle breeze.

What was it his sister was toying with? Dark, uneven pieces that looked like leather and metal and a leather rod she was moving among them, counting or bewitching, as if a wand or a school pointer. She would not be going to school, no more than he would anymore, in spite of his mother's wishes. Buck snorted, and the kid looked back to the ironing board and beside it the small coal stove, the iron heating upon it, and beside and below that the man reclining on the grass, up on his elbows, the corked bottle fallen to its side near his finger tips. He saw him push up, as if to rise, then slump back into the grass again. Completely drunk now, he thought. His

24

mother was reaching above, pulling the pins from a sheet. Then Mr. Jones had struggled to his knees, one hand in the grass to keep himself steady. He was looking down the lawn to where the kid's sister had raised the rod up and was tapping the objects hard, the ones between her knees and a longer pliable thing on the quilt beside her. He could hear Buck breathing at his side, attentive now as he was, as they both saw Mr. Jones climb up to his feet and stagger. He was bellowing and swearing, twisting to find his wife, who had turned at the sound, the sheet blown to wrap around her body. Then he found her, and the kid saw his arm come up to jab and point to where his sister had stopped tapping the objects, hearing him too, and had turned to look back over her shoulder.

"She got my whip and tack!" He growled the words, but they were distinct, vicious and frustrated, and he was looking around for something, frantically, then saw the iron on the stove top and grabbed at it and started down the lawn in jerky strides. The kid's mother was after him, but was tripping in the sheet and falling, and he looked to see his sister climb up to her stubby legs, knowing what was coming. She started running, but she could only move slowly. Then he was on his feet and Buck was already gone. He saw the dog reach and down the little girl, then grab her in his jaws at her nape and lift her, her feet dragging on the lawn as he pulled and carried her toward the woods. The man was quickly approaching them, the hot, heavy iron shaking in his fist, and it was all that the kid could do to call out, something, he didn't know what. His mother was on her feet again, hands in the air, striking her breast, and Mr. Jones had turned and seen him and was heading up the slope toward the barn. He was quieter now and seemed even sober, and he was coming on, the iron swinging in his hand at his side. The kid glanced beyond him toward the woods, but Buck and his sister were gone. Then he judged the distance to the barn door and saw he couldn't make it. But his mother was screaming now, and though the man kept coming at him, he glanced over his shoulder, altering his drunken course, giving him the moment. The kid ran to the barn door then and ducked inside, crossed the dirt floor, passing the basket of peaches, and stepped over the sill of the low back window. He was running then, behind the barn and around its far side, heading for the lawn and the safety of the woods beyond. He looked back once. He couldn't see his mother or Mr. Jones. The white sheet floated like a cloud on the grass.

"I came to a clearing a few hundred yards into the woods, a place where the canopy of leaves was so thick that the sun couldn't nourish the lower branches and trees had died and fallen over and become mulch. It was there I found the ripped away collar of her little dress and the blood stains on it and found what I thought was one of the burred tassels from the whip's end. I wanted to call out for Buck, but I was afraid of what the sound might bring. I searched the clearing carefully, finding nothing more, then headed on deeper, to where the light failed into a premature dusk and the moss-covered ground grew spongy, its decayed scent bringing the safety of foreignness to my nose. It was only after I'd wended my way deep into the wood for a good half-mile that I came upon Buck again, but not my sister.

"He was backed in under a fallen branch, and I saw first those steady dark eyes that had been a warning to many. His massive head moved, distinguishing itself among the shadows, that implacable expression of pure concentration, ominous and ready. He was scanning the near distance, and I saw his ears perk at the sound of my footfalls and I whispered his name. A quiet whine then, his mouth opening, that pink tongue lolling out to the side in a smile and panting, and he became old Buck again, my friendly pup.

"We searched in the woods for a good two hours, until darkness had fallen completely. Then we lay down beside each other and could hear night birds and the rustlings of small forest animals as we sunk into sleep. There were no dreams for me, not of my mother or sister, or of Mr. Jones, but I don't know about Buck. In the morning we woke early, in the first hint of light dappling the fallen leaves and began our search again.

"Buck would pick up the scent at times and head out with resolve, but he always came to confusion, standing beside deadfall or in some clearing. He'd be shaking his head and looking around quizzically, as if searching now for his lost abilities, and what little I had, gathered from the tracking of deer in winter, came also to nothing. We found brackish water where the woods descended into swamp and drank sparingly from it. We found robbed nests and abandoned burrows and a dead baby owl, but we found no evidence of my sister, and when I looked deep into Buck's eyes for her recent history there was nothing there either. Her blood stained collar and the whip's tip, that was all that seemed left of her, and finally, in the recognition of our failure, we tracked up out of the wood's depths to the far side, where the trees grew stunted and there were rolling hills and farms and wood houses. We came then to what passed for a town, only a general store, gas station, and church. Buck sat in the dirt as I went in to beg for food and to tell my story. And that's where they took and shackled me, there at the counter while I was explaining my problems to the old man."

→THREE←

The El Capitan was a late arrival from Los Angeles, and by the time the porter had lugged my suitcases to the compartment and I'd laid out my night clothes, darkness was falling. I could see the lights of the city through the large viewing window once the train had left the station. Then there was only desert, a shadowy moonscape under the illuminated heaven of blinking stars. I sat back in the cushy seat and lit up the pipe, a vice I allowed myself only on certain occasions.

It was probable that Mr. Jones had killed the kid's mother with the heavy iron and that, a few weeks later, Buck had disposed of Mr. Jones. There was no real proof in either case, but the authorities had assumed the latter. They'd found him on the porch behind the tapered columns, his throat ripped out, and they had found bits of fur among the shards of glass from the broken bottle.

Buck was gone by the time they brought the kid out in shackles, but the kid could see the impression of his body in dust at the road's edge where he had lain. Beyond that was open farm country, and he watched the dozen men engaged in awkward tracking as they walked slowly through the fields. Then they were out of sight and he was on the bench in the paddy wagon, moving toward a destination that materialized as a county jail. It was there they beat him, then questioned him about the whereabouts of his sister, and where he learned of his mother's death, most probably, they said, from a fainting fall as she'd watched the dog attack her daughter and carry her away. She'd struck her head against the coal stove, they thought. Now the little girl was gone, the kid under some vague suspicion, and Mr. Jones could claim the farm and house and all the material goods and any money.

The bowl of my pipe, a meerschaum with a long stem, the head of some bearded patriarch carved into it, had grown cold. I tamped down the Cuban tobacco, then lit it up again. Sleep seemed far away, even though I'd changed into my silk pajamas and the train rocked like a child's carriage. Outside, the night was narcotic, and I avoided that view and all thoughts of Wisconsin and my arrival. This was not difficult, lost as I was in recovering memory of the kid and our increasingly drunken conversations just two nights ago in Naco. I remembered I'd asked him about his first escape and that he'd said he'd just walked out of the place. Then, full of tequila, beans and beer, I'd brought up the subject of the others, recognizing my inappropriateness immediately.

"That's professional, isn't it?" he had said. The subject was dropped and we'd continued our drinking well into the morning hours as he'd told his story. He knew nothing of Buck now, not for two years, and he assumed that he was dead and gone.

The Christians had awakened early. He could hear their singing through the church wall where he'd slept among oleander bushes the night of his first escape. Then Buck was there, poking his nose against the kid's blood-stained trousers, and as the singing rose to crescendo the two stole away in dawn's first light.

It had taken him a few weeks to figure the way out, and in that time they'd continued to accuse him. Mr. Jones had come, not to see him, but to fuel the fire of suspicion. He'd heard his voice, sober at that time, down the row of cells where the office door had stood open. Later they'd told him of the man's death and that he'd be there a while longer. They'd beaten him a few more times, but without heart. Then he'd left, knowing for certain that this would be a new offense and a legitimate one. It became in a while the only one, growing more serious for them in its repeated occasions and as his celebrity increased.

He and Buck headed south, through Kansas, the northeastern tip of Oklahoma and into Arkansas as winter came and the effects of the Great Depression settled in. They came upon families in old pickup trucks, piled high to the sideboards with possessions, and those on foot, singly and in groups that might have been family, though some were ominous, a certain hunger and the will to act upon it by whatever means were available in their thin faces. They camped with some of them, along rivers and near railroad yards, sharing potatoes and boiled cabbage, stolen chickens and feral cats that looked like chicken meat in the soup pot among bits of carrots and onions from which the earth rot had been cut away. Once they lingered too long with a troop of tramps, and four tried to take his shoes and leather belt in the night. Buck saved him that time, alerting him and standing them off until he could rise from his bed of bug-infested straw and get away.

Then they entered Louisiana, above Shreveport, and came into different country between there and Natchitoches not far from the Red River, swamp land where they found themselves protected from people in unsavory circumstance, kept company only by insects and snakes, with catfish for their dinners, and were alone, and afterwards it seemed like fate that had brought them there, for they were very near the prison of brutality and suicide, and the kid was taken again before long, an escapee now, and Buck was gone away as before.

He told me little of that prison's particulars, though he warned me of its Draconian system. It was three o'clock in the morning by then. The cowboys and the old man had long ago departed, to be replaced by two weary whores who had wandered down the boardwalk once the Casa Rojo and the other place had closed down for the night. They sat at a table, their eyes absently urging us until they found we had no interest in their profession. They seemed relieved then and turned to their lazy eating, sipping at the strong black coffee and yawning, bean mush visible among bits of tan tortilla in their open mouths.

We slept what remained of the night in a sagging double bed in a room behind the bar's kitchen. The bartender made the arrangements, then surely proceeded with his betrayal of us. Or maybe it was the prostitutes or the cowboys, or even the old man in the bib overalls. The room smelled of burnt beans and rancid oil. It was small, about the size of that metal shed at the prison. We slept beside each other, exhausted and half drunk, yet the kid continued his talking, and at one point, close to dawn, his resolve gone away for a while, he related in detail the terms of one of his escapes. We fell asleep after that, and I think I remember him turning, my own movement toward him until I had formed into a chair and he was sitting in it.

I awakened in dawn's light at the window and could hear whispers and the movements of furniture beyond the wall, and I knew they were coming for him. I rose then, leaving the kid sleeping in the randy bed, and dressed quickly, then slipped out the door into baking heat and a town that could hold no romance or mystery once it became starkly apparent in bright morning sun.

Danker was waiting beside the Packard in front of Union Station, and I lifted my hand in greeting as I walked out into the humid morning air. I watched as he helped the porter load the suitcases into the trunk, tipped him, and climbed in behind the wheel. I sat in the front seat beside him as he worked his way through the city streets, heading for the main road that would take us to Wisconsin. It would be a long trip, eight hours at least before we arrived at the house north of Hayward, and in the beginning of our journey we caught up on things. The Louisiana prison plans had arrived, and he'd brought them along. Once we'd reached the highway and he could relax a little in his driving, I told him the story of the kid.

Danker is twenty years older than I, fifty-five, but fit and alert, an outdoorsman who had continued to work for my father after my mother's death in nineteen-fourteen, when I was frisky and troublesome and fourteen too.

My father never cared much for women. My mother was a convenience to him, and when she was gone he'd hired Danker to take her place as secretary, house manager, and companion. I'd tested him in my adolescence, and he had been motherly and understanding, never pushing, but guiding me in values and the riches of ideas and nature in ways my father never had. When my father died when I was twenty-two and away at college, Danker stayed on, and so did Count Southpaw, his sister Bret and his two daughters.

Count was a master gardener, a distinguished and formal man, and was sixty-three years old. He'd come up into Wisconsin from Florida before the turn of the century, after his wife was murdered and he was left with a sister and two little girls to care for when he was only twenty-five. He'd been a baseball pitcher in an early version of the Negro League, earning money through gambling on his skills in games with small town teams throughout the South. Once in a backwater in Georgia his team's tent-city was attacked by rednecks and the players had been severely beaten. When the marauders left, he'd checked his family, only to find his girls weeping at his wife's side, her head caved in and resting in a pool of blood.

The girls were in their early forties now, Virgo and Tallahas-see, and liked to be called *the girls*. Both were tall and stately and looked as if they had just stepped out of some country in Africa. They were beautiful, learned women, and I'd spent many hours in conversation with them. Neither Count Southpaw, Bret, nor the girls chose often to stay in the house overnight, though they had their own rooms there on the upper floor. They liked to sleep in their cottage beside the river near Hayward, in the comfort of their own beds. Count and Bret, like Danker, worked at the house full time, and Tal and Virg came over on days when Bret needed their help. Danker hired day laborers for heavy work when they were needed, but it was these five who kept the house and grounds in proper order on a daily basis.

"Has the world changed?" I asked. "I've been busy."

We'd passed Beloit by then. There were few cars on the road, and before too long we'd be coming to Madison and beyond that the first edges of wilderness.

"Well, Roosevelt," he said. "That Social Security business? It got passed in Congress. And Will Rogers. You heard about that? He died in a plane crash in Alaska."

"Yes," I said. The sad news even in Arizona. "But that's good, I mean the Social Security. It *should* be good."

"People are still on the move."

"How many?"

"About two dozen since you left. Bret's kept the chili and soup going, plenty of bread too. And I've put some men on day work, hauling out brush and deadfall."

"Just people," I said.

"Right," he said. "Most of the opportunists won't get this far north. But come winter, we'll have to be watchful again. Those break-ins for the warmth."

"That's right," I said.

"And there's something else. Avery Brattle called again."

"How many times?"

"Well, three at least. I finally told him when you'd be coming back, but that you'd be leaving right away again."

"Persistent bastard. Next time I'm going to set him straight."

"Language," he said.

Once past Madison, we stopped for gas and to relieve ourselves. Danker had brought sandwiches and iced tea. We sat at a wooden bench in a small grove of trees beyond the station's side. I could smell the pine needles and the turned earth in a farm field out of sight beyond. The scents would be stronger when we were past Eau Claire. I was ready for home again, and soon we were back on the road, Danker at the wheel and I in the back seat going over the Louisiana prison renderings and the map they'd sent along with them to give me some sense of surroundings. There seemed to be no significant towns for miles around, only swamp and small elevated islands of tropic growth. "Quicksand" was noted in a few places, and there were even small drawings of alligators here and there. It looked like a tourist map. I didn't trust its accuracy at all.

The warden himself had called to state the problem. I'd noted an inarticulate rage even as he spoke of things in a measured way. Rage at the fact that they still had escapes even though they were quite confident in their methods and had increased the brutality, and with it the attendant suicides. "Not often, mind you, but enough." When I'd asked how many, he'd grudgingly given me the figure, one every three months or so, which was a very large number for maximum security, even though there were three hundred desperate souls in the place. I started to ask if they had any ideas, but thought better of it. No need to fuel his frustration. They surely didn't. Why else would they be calling me? Then we'd made our arrangements.

The renderings were drawings made to scale, those executed when the prison had been fashioned from the ruined stone mansion it had been shortly before the turn of the century. What they depicted was no more than a renovation project, albeit an extensive one. They'd left the curving stone walls intact on both stories, so that none of the rooms was symmetrical; some were pie shaped, others oval, and the building contained many alcoves and turret-like chambers. On the ground level, at the stone perimeter, someone had penned in the dimensions of cleared ground, a hundred yards in a half circle, and, beyond that, heavy growth and swampland. In one place, in the manner of a doorway on architects' blueprints, the opening to the single road that was the only way out. This was where much of the chain gang work took place, the road constantly threatened by overgrowth and washout. The prisoners were used to clear and repair it in shifts that worked throughout the day and night. Torch lights and sufficient guards. And they were, after all, chained, the warden had assured me. They'd lost no one in that circumstance.

There was something odd about the drawings, for though they were careful and clear in their depiction, when it came to the back side of the prison they faded out into a haziness beyond a jagged line that seemed to be some kind of divider. There were things there, but they were insubstantial and I couldn't make them out.

The original castle had been the antebellum folly of a German viscount who had come to America with money and an exploitative plan for the use of slaves in a mining venture. Most probably syphilitic and surely decadent, given the stories of bacchanals once the castle had been built and was his home, the viscount had succumbed to heart attack in his early sixties. After that the castle had laid waste, its furniture and fixtures carried away by those willing to brave the road in and the trip out with heavy and awkward burdens over the years. The warden had told me this story, growing quite garrulous in its relation. The viscount's life had become a dark and romanticized myth, something to account for the mystery the place still seemed to hold, for the prisoners, of course, bewildered and brutalized as they were, but for the officials too.

A cornucopia of scent now as we passed beyond Hayward, fish, maple sap, and the burn of saws in wood; these melded with other familiars in a hint of fall breeze at the window, though it was still August. The mile-long drive then, lined with stately pines, my home at the end of it.

While Danker unloaded the car and took the suitcases up to my room and set about the preparation of dinner, I strolled the grounds, inhaling the sweet air and taking note of the order of flowering plants and shrubs. My father had been no horticulture fan, but had thought a garden was proper. He'd put in gravel walkways beyond the large clay parking area below the porch, topiary beside elevated perennial beds and mirroring ponds with lily pads and golden garibaldi, all laid out in severe rectangles in the manner of something he'd noted as aristocratic in a book. He'd even had a maze constructed, of juniper taller than I was, and it was beyond that where the trail began that led up to the cabin.

My father had been wise about land, having earned most of his money in logging, and had accumulated eight hundred acres of it. The house was built near the center, three sprawling stories, behind which were the stables and green-houses, the former empty now, but the latter burgeoning under Count Southpaw's hands, full of his seedlings and plant experiments. I'd reduced the garden's size after my father's death, and no longer was a crew necessary for its maintenance. It was the Count's domain now, and it grew lush and healthy. He kept the maze trimmed, its narrow, serpentine pathways in good order. He'd established a large vegetable garden beyond the unused stables, between them and the beginning of the northern forest. All our vegetables and herbs came from there, his garden fruitful from early spring well into the beginning of winter. There were fruit trees as well, apple and peach and two small mangoes struggling with the climate in an orchard to the garden's side. I picked the fruit, together with the help of Tallahassee and Virgo. Bret baked the pies, and we all ate them.

Danker was standing on the broad porch, a frosty martini in his hand. Dusk was coming on, turning the pine needles silver.

"Here you are," he said. "Dinner in fifteen?"

It was bluegill and crappies sautéed in butter, and small red potatoes in parsley and butter, fiddle heads, a salad of mixed greens, and a slightly chilled Condrieu. We spoke only casually as we ate, subjects with soft edges, neither wanting to disturb the succulence. Danker had kept the lights low in the massive dining room where my father had entertained his business associates opulently. There were candles burning on the long table, and we sat together near its end, our feet in slippers on the plush carpet.

"It's good to be home," I said at one point.

"What about tomorrow? Are there any plans?"

"There's going to be trout for dinner, I can tell you that. I'm going fishing."

Once dinner was finished and I'd helped Danker with the dishes, I went up to my room to read and prepare for bed. It was the same room I'd slept in as a child, and though I'd introduced adult furniture and had expanded the closet space to accommodate my extensive wardrobe, there were still childish things about: my tattered teddy bear, bits of high school paraphernalia, year books stacked beside college texts. I'd studied in Chicago, architecture at the University, but had found the way into my current profession on my own. There had been no profession of that kind, until I'd invented it.

I slept in a long monogrammed night shirt. I was naked under it, and after I'd turned the light off, then turned on my side, I felt the fleeting presence of the kid, as if he were there in the dark and was shifting his hips to slide back toward me, to come and sit in that chair my body had made ready for him.

I awoke before the blush of first light, dressed myself in old familiar clothes, then headed down the broad staircase and into the foyer, which was the size of a hotel lobby. It was part of my father's idea of a proper opulence, like the pool room he'd insisted upon, a place for manly drink and the smoking of cigars. Then I was out the door, through the twisting passages of the maze, and was heading up the overgrown trail that would take me to the cabin.

The trail had not always been so. My father had made a broad and gentle passage for the half-mile trip, using the cabin as a hunting and fishing lodge. There he would entertain business associates, men who at times had been fat and out of shape though imagined themselves as ready for anything, as they were in business. The cabin itself, amply outfitted for comfort, was in part designed to prevent any disabuse of this adolescent illusion.

The cabin was mine now, a private place, and I'd let nature loose on the trail so that it would no longer be a welcoming passage to others. Both Bret and Danker went there occasionally, to clean and stock it, but they were careful to leave no traces. Once I'd reached the door and entered, then lit an oil lamp and adjusted the wick, I was presented only with the familiar: the overstuffed chairs, the scent of knotty pine, and my ice- and fly-fishing poles neat in their rack on the wall beside the fourteen-point buck's head.

I brewed strong coffee, and while it steeped I went to the large marble bathroom and washed up. The bathroom had been my father's indulgence, totally inappropriate in this seemingly rough and ready place. He'd made a joke of it, as he often had when it came to the four comfortable bedrooms, one of which I'd converted into a study where I did most of my paperwork and reading. There was a room with a back entrance into the rear yard and the woods behind. It was there that fish were cleaned. There were high pole racks in the yard for dressing deer.

Light dappled the furniture as the sun rose and filtered its way through the pines. When I'd finished the coffee and the horsing up of my fly rod gear, I headed out and down a winding narrow trail that would take me to the lake and around it.

My father had named Blue Lake, though it was not blue but faintly yellow in summer when pine pollen formed powdery patterns on its surface. When I reached its shore I saw the ice fishing shack, pulled up and resting at a slight tilt on the strip of sandy soil at lake's edge. The door was latched, but not locked, and once I'd entered and glimpsed the compact and ordered surroundings, the four circular holes in the floor, the benches beside them, I could tell that others had been there. They'd been neat and respectful, but there were head indentations in the two cot pillows, and someone, a child perhaps, had forgotten something, a ragged and threadbare cloth on the floor near a bench leg. I owned a lot of land, and Danker had a periodic schedule for exploring it, but once the Depression had settled in we'd come to agree that we would give no trouble to wanderers, so long as there was no violation and no one tried for the cabin. There were other structures on the land as well, old root cellars, dilapidated barns and machine storage sheds, and Danker gave them a wide birth, only checking their condition when they were clearly unoccupied.

I looked down at the four holes, recalling the lake's name, that luminous starlight blue in the walls of the two-foot ice shafts. Slush would form on the lake's surface as it began to freeze again. There was a metal dipper for lifting it out. Then the surface, seen as a circle at the end of a brief tunnel, would be clear again. I'd wait, my bait at the end of a short pole. Then a yellow bluegill would drift by, suspended as if in glycerine, trails of thin weed, and below, the darker athletic shape of a great northern. I loved ice fishing, as I loved the fly rod, and though I know that in my child-hood my father had taken me into those magical worlds without begrudging the intrusion, I could remember no real enthusiasm in him. My memories were of Danker as the one who had taught me the skills and pleasures.

It was six by the time I reached the river and made my way to the trout spot, a pattern of eddying pools where the river turned and widened below rapids. A few large boulders rose above the surface, lichen covered. Willows hung well out from the bank, their weeping branches so low that under the weight of dew their tips touched and were dampened. It was light now, but the willows spread their shadows on the dimly shimmering surface in just the right places, and I was quick with my hip-waders and was into the river almost to my thighs, casting my first casts, before sun shifted in the branches. A trout struck immediately, but I was not ready for such quick results and I missed him, then settled into the rhythms of my casting. The fly would plunk down without sound, and I would gently jig it into life as it drifted near reeds on the river's far side.

I fished for two hours, and when I felt a tiredness in my shoulder and knew I'd had enough, I worked my way through the current and struggled up to a rock shelf at the river's edge. I'd caught seven fish and had kept three large trout in the creel, enough for dinner. Once I'd stripped away the rubber outfit, then packed the rod and gear, I took my shirt off, sat down and watched the river's eddies in the sun, giving myself up to vision rather than thought. The surface was hypnotic, but the fixed boulders kept me from drifting out of focus. The patterns of light cast through the willows constantly shifted as their limbs rocked slowly in a breeze. I could see sparrows flitting at the shore, an occasional monarch in dipping flight. The sun was drying the lichen, and on the rock boulders too there was pattern, quilt-like, and in one of the quilt's materializing squares was a pin point of brighter light, something glittering. What is that, I thought, then knew what it was and reached to my left earlobe, felt the diamond stud, and laughed to myself. I'd left it in, all the way from Tucson on the train, and now I left my vision of the river and its peacefulness and gave thought to that other life, as if it were not mine at all, but only some masquerade.

I'd had my ear pierced in Guinea, when I'd been brought there to aid in the construction of a penal colony. It was early on in my career, but not before a few idiosyncratic solutions that had brought me a little celebrity and a reputation for oddness, which I quickly learned to cultivate. When I returned to the states I bought the diamond stud to replace the bone hook the native merchant had installed, a very small diamond in an almost invisible setting, yet immediately apparent when I wore it, which I did only when I was consulting.

I'm tall, about five foot nine or nine and a half, and have a swarthy complexion that I inherited from my mother, who was part gypsy, or at least liked to let that myth of exotica into conversation. My hair, like hers, has a certain wiriness and sheen. I have black eyes, the irises dark as the pupils, and when I smile, which is seldom when I'm consulting, I like to keep it tentative and enig-matic.

The men I work for, with few exceptions, are ignorant and crude. They know about prisons, at least the one they work in, but only through their own short-sighted experience. The diamond stud helps, if nothing more than in avoidance of their society out-side of work. Some, I'm sure, think me a homosexual, but beyond the kind they've rigidly defined for their own safety. The diamond makes them feel uncomfortable, and this is exactly what I want.

→FOUR←

They brought the kid down from the truck bed with the others, all chained together at the ankles and they could not stride properly. It was humid there and sticky, below Shreveport in swamp country, close to the prison of brutality and suicide. The others were black mostly, their heads were down, and they had no shoulders to speak of and their arms came out it seemed at the sides of their necks. The guards took the chains away, and then they stood at the sides of the road with their guns and watched the men as they levered up rocks, leaving deep holes, which they filled with sand and stone using shovels. Some hacked away with curved knives at brush and thick vines that had grown into the road. A man came in a car and got out and watched them for a while, then spoke to the others and got in the car again and left. They drank water from a wooden dipper. A guard stepped forward from the roadside on occasion and beat some of the black ones and a white one, not the kid. His whip was large as the kind used for horses, who were much larger than the shoulderless men and had four legs and could stand steady. The men lost their two knees and fell to the ground, where the guard continued to whip their backs and legs until he stopped doing that for a while. Then the prisoners sat in the truck bed, their legs hanging down. They ate something, then went back to working in the road.

The kid knew Buck was there, up the hill in the deep brush, watching him. In a while, when it was getting dark, they chained the men again and urged them onto the truck bed and left. Then other men came, also in chains, and set to work like the ones who had left, the kid among them, only now it was dark, and the men with the guns lit bright torches.

Buck had left when they'd brought the kid out through the store door, in chains then too, and with the old man in his apron following. He had been at a distance when they took him away in the wagon. Then he'd headed back for the woods where he'd lost the little girl, sniffed around for a while, a few days, but there was nothing and he'd gone beyond the woods and up the short grass to the house to find the kid, but he wasn't there. Mr. Jones was, and he had lifted an axe to kill him, and Buck had ripped his throat out then and had left and gone back to the store where they'd taken the kid away. He'd picked up the scent, then followed it to a building with bars on the windows. He'd waited there, and when nothing had happened but a growing hunger, he'd found a place near there among others of his kind who were rovers, six of them, with him seven, and they knocked over garbage cans and rooted for grubs under tree branches and stole chickens from wire enclosures and even chewed at carrots and potatoes that they dug up out of meager gardens.

They slept in the fields where the grasses were higher than they were, not all at once, for there were always those who were not tired and continued roving, and in the mornings, just as the sun rose and while people were still sleeping, they moved silently in a loose pack, taking what was available, until one of their number was shot in the head by a farmer while stealing from a basket of tubers on a low sill. After that they were careful and less playful in their meanderings. It was Depression now, and the people were growing desperate, just as they were, and there was little left to be counted on for expected responses.

Then Buck had found the kid again, under oleander bushes beside a church building where people were singing in the early morning, and they had left there on a long and at times interesting journey.

They passed wagons with people in them and on foot beside them. They'd been attacked by people wanting something. It had grown hotter, then the weather had changed, and it had grown cool at night in places where they heard the sounds of animals that were unfamiliar. They found food and lodging in ruined buildings and in wilderness where the trees were stunted and covered in strange foliage and vines. Finally they found a place where the earth was wet and spongy under their feet and had holed up there for a while. Then men had come and taken the kid away again, and Buck headed out, on his own again, and had come to a place in a swamp where a man walked with a stick and a woman threw scraps of food in the yard for him and for the others who had scented her out too. There was fighting among them, but he'd killed only one of them. The others had stared in his eyes and then lowered their tails. They'd rolled over on their backs then and pissed into the air. After that they avoided him or followed him with their heads down, their muzzles close to his shoulder, and softly whining. There were females among them and he'd fucked a few of them because it was his nature, then had left that place and had found the prison of brutality and suicide and the kid's scent again.

It was night, his second one, and the trouble now was small flying insects that aimed for his eyes, but he blinked them away and kept watch. He could smell the kid still, but not near, or if he was near he was covered in other scent and seemed far away. Then he saw him, but not him, a figure different from the human shape. He was coming across the same ground where the men had worked in the road the night before, drifting strangely in starlight, the sway of a beam of light behind him and a man behind the light, running, holding a rifle and waving it in various directions.

The kid whistled. Then Buck was coming at the man from the side to down him. He got one eye and a hand, then took his knee in his jaws and crushed it and the man began to roll on the ground yelling. He could have had the rest of him easily, but the kid called him away, and once he was beside him and the thin clothing had been gathered from the air, they'd left that place, climbing the embankment of thick growth, and had moved on until they were back once again in the wilderness and were making their way north into cooler weather.

⇥FIVE⇤

The train fell to its knees in the yard beyond the station leaving Shreveport. I felt a lurch and saw the boar bristle brush and bone comb fall from the narrow shelf to clatter when I looked up from my reading, then heard the long whistle shriek and the muffled sounds of running in the passage beyond my compartment door. I was feeling for the comb and brush when my fingers hit something that had slid under the heater vent, a scissors-like object, but stranger. When I brought it out from under and up into the light at the window, I recognized it was an eyelash curler. Some Southern belle, I thought, the object among her many accoutrements, carelessly dropped and forgotten. It looked like a device to be used in the torture of small children. Now the train had fallen too, its engine wheels off track at a missed switch. I'd be stuck in Shreveport, where sticky summer was still in full power and would be late for my appointment at the prison of brutality and suicide.

Those of us who had compartments were put up at a hotel nearby. The others were given meal chits and set to their own devices. I saw what I thought were a few of them among the milling homeless with vacant faces in the station when I passed through. There were no taxi cabs, but I found a willing porter to wheel my suitcases over the hot steamy streets. When I got to the hotel I called the prison and was connected to the warden. He said he'd send a car in the morning, I should be ready by seven. I might try the catfish, at a restaurant whose name he gave me.

Sundered from my travel, I was itchy and had no brain for reading. The room was sticky, the air still and soporific. I knew I couldn't stay put there; still, where to go and what to wear? I could smell oil and the burn of metals in friction from the station's yard, and on the small city map the hotel provided I found a body of water, a small lake at the center of a park within walking distance, though a long walk to be sure.

It was well into afternoon by the time I set forth, yet the sun was still bright and flooding down oppressively, and after a few blocks trudging down ruined sidewalks cluttered with human desperation, I found a dime store and bought a baseball cap to match my grey cotton shirt and to keep the sun's heat back. People rested on the sidewalks and on benches, some under broad umbrellas, others under canopies fashioned from a gathering of broken and discarded ones, men together, women and men, and at times families. No hands reached out begging, but eyes did, and not for food or money, but in quiet desperation for an answer that couldn't be formulated. I looked away, quite aware that I was doing that, and thought again of opening the unused servants' quarters at the rear of the house when I returned home, aware too of the way such thought was salving the unspecifiable guilt I was feeling just then. Roosevelt: I forced up a romantic generality of hope. Then I left the broken sidewalks and these people of various ages, though a generation now in their common extremity, and came to the park's edge and at its center the small lake, whereabout no evidence of the Depression lingered on the walkways or cherry wood benches to present an eyesore to the old and satisfied gothic houses that claimed ownership of the park's view.

Policemen strolled the walks with dark dogs in tow. Old women sat on lakeside benches under parasols in fine, white linen. There were no children or quick-paced adults, but a faint breeze and the scent of lemon trees rode the lake's ripples. I took an empty bench on the downwind side, bathed in the coolness of drying sweat at my arms and collar, and gave myself up for a while to memory.

The kid had revealed the terms of that one escape in the early morning hours in Naco. It was not so much its details as the part it played in his myth and reputation as a master of disguise and misdirection that seemed the important thing. The myth itself was misdirection. In looking for his inventiveness, they had tendency to miss the awkward and mundane and, not the least of it, the help of others. His reputation followed him: a seemingly sweet young man, but a brilliant loner. Nothing would be what it seemed to be.

He'd been close to exhaustion and had drunk beer and tequila and we'd had a long, civilized, conversation. It was also the case that I was the only one who might fully appreciate his abilities. We were in the same game, after all, though on different sides of the table. In our time together I'd come to trust him and to desire a closeness to him that I, and he too, had acted upon in that filthy little room. I'd made a chair for him, and he'd come to sit in it.

This is what he'd done, at first as an intentionally thwarted dry run, in a prison outside Woodward, Oklahoma. He'd spent a few weeks stretching and, though quite thin already, losing weight.

Initially he'd been caught with an extra prison uniform and a carved block of wood with strands of human hair glued onto it. They of course figured a plan to use his cell bed, some kind of stuffing, and that he'd seem to be there while he was somewhere else, in a tunnel or sewer pipe, or on some circuitous secret route that would take him through the shadows of buildings, even as the beams of their search lights played over the yard and shone against windows, below which he crept, the sounds of his motion and breathing unapparent in the noise of guard whistles, rifle shots and sirens, all pelted by a pounding rain or in starlight as in moving pictures under the faint, theatrical glow of a full moon. Such drama, because their lives were empty of drama and they could not imagine it beyond cinema and the lurid crime magazines they read for the pictures in them. Their prisoners planned, suffered and died around them, operating in a rich matrix of human relations, betrayals, and subtle plots. But it was only when the kid came to them, in his mystery and reputation, that they found a taste for such complexity, and that wobbled what little reason they were capable of and worked perfectly to his advantage.

He managed with the help of others who felt privileged to be involved in one of the kid's great escapes, and while the authorities buttressed security at the walls and at every suspicious turning and hiding place they could imagine, he gathered his materials in various caches, continued with his stretching exercises, and waited for death. They had searched his cell thoroughly and had checked the locks and bars. They kept a close watch on him, but they did not violate his physical person nor privacy in sleep or evacuation. They wanted to stop his escape, to gain their own celebrity in doing that, but not his attempt. Otherwise, there'd be no escape to prevent. They gave him room, as others had done elsewhere, and since their focus was on him exclusively, a little bit of room was all he needed. That, and at times Buck, but not this time.

Once again the false figure in the cell bed, this time a casting fashioned from a wrapping of plaster-impregnated Ace bandages, just a torso, no legs or arms, as the warden himself saw when he threw back the blanket, then sounded the full alarm. The head was the shape of a head only, a nose complete with nostrils, but no other features. The hair may have been the kid's hair, just bits at the crown, the rest of the head-shape darkened by shoe blacking to appear as hair in the shadowy light of the cell.

An old man had died, from a heart attack followed by a fall in the yard the day before, and after the warden had arranged for the photographic record and had ordered a guard stationed at the kid's cell bed, he went himself to the infirmary where the body remained, refrigerated and awaiting transport to a medical school for use in student dissections. There he found the moulages, not open wounds in the old man's face and shoulder, but rubber applique, a fake of severe injury, and surely the kid's work.

Still, the man was dead and was not the kid. The warden called out the doctor and made absolutely sure of that through medical examination, and only after a thorough search of the pharmacy and attendant rooms, cells and storage places, did he release the body, ordering also that the medical school transport be searched from top to bottom when it arrived the following day. He'd ordered a complete lockdown, guards at the outer walls and even beyond as soon as the fake kid had been discovered in the cell bed, and though his heart had sunk at the thought of the six or more hours between last bed check and the discovery, which was too much time, he had his men set about searching the entire prison with great care. They found nothing.

What they did find they found the next day, but only after the medical school transport had taken the body of the old man away. Word had been leaked to the press, and they'd covered the false kid with the blanket again and lowered the lights to approximate the night and the effectiveness of the ruse so that they could not be blamed so easily for the mistaken identity.

The guard stood at the bedside, and the reporters and photographers crowded the cell so that the warden had to shoulder his way among them in the flashes of camera bulbs and questions. Then he threw the blanket back again and revealed the split open carcass of the plaster torso, inside of which were indentations holding a half-eaten apple, a few carrots, and a mason jar full of urine, all bathed in a scent of chloroform and a faint light entering through the nostril holes fashioned for breathing. There were cups near the head in the front side of the split cocoon where the kid's tucked up knees had impressed themselves. He'd needed another person to wrap him up, but he did not speak of that to me, only of the limbering success of his exercises. Imbedded in the plaster of the concave curves that had gripped the shallow moons of his buttocks were two words cut from a Ouija board, *hello*, *goodbye*, one left and one right and both blinking, he remembered, in the flashes of bulbs and shutter clicks.

"He ordered me home, a week without pay for my incompetence." These were the kid's whispered words, there in the early morning in Naco. He'd stood in the cell at the bed's side, in uniform and makeup and blackened hair, and even now he had to chuckle when he thought of the chloroformed, naked guard and imagined the warden's expression when he was discovered, pressed back into the wall below the narrow bed. He'd hoped the photographers had returned again. The old man's moulages had been a diversion only, and I wondered then, sitting in the park and rehearsing it, if the whole story and the kid's willingness to tell it had been a diversion too, for my benefit, against the time when we might find ourselves in contact once again.

→SIX←

I was waiting in the hotel lobby when I saw the Buick pull up and park in the loading zone. Two men got out, both dressed in tan summer suits, almost identical in height, weight and oiled hair. They stood on the steamy sidewalk looking down at my suitcases and talking to the porter. Something transpired, and the passenger headed for the glass doors pulling a large checkered handkerchief from his pocket and mopping his brow as I was rising. The other opened the car's trunk lid and supervised the porter's struggle as he loaded my satchels.

"You're Pollard?" the man said.

He was tall as I was, but fat and thick through chest and shoulders, and his ill fitting and rumpled suit showed sweat stains at the collar. Rather than answer I lifted my briefcase and extended it toward him. He looked at it, considering for a moment only, then took it, and I followed him to the doors and out into the morning heat, noticing how the crotch of his pants hung down almost to his knees.

They sat beside each other in the front seat and I was in the back. The car's interior smelled of decaying flesh, sickeningly apparent under the strong sweet scent of artificial wintergreen, and the hot and unrelieving breeze at the window once we'd left the city only strengthened it. I could see the sheen of oil on their necks below their haircut lines.

"What *is* that smell?" I asked and saw the one in the passenger seat turn toward the other.

"Jimmy, do you smell anything?"

"No," Jimmy said.

"He don't smell anything," the other said, looking straight ahead again.

We traveled along a dead-straight highway for an hour or more, fallow fields to either side and in the far, heat haze distance on the left what looked like dusty trees billowing. We passed occasional encampments, wagons and rusted cars, slow moving people in clothing that was the faded color of the land itself. At each one the passenger touched the driver lightly on his shoulder, pointed and said things I could not hear. Then we slowed and turned off to the left and were descending down a narrow dirt road where we were soon shaded under drooping willows and wild oak, vines snaking thickly on their trunks and branches, moss hanging from them almost to the rough shoulder. After another hour, when the road narrowed in the encroachment of growth thick as a wall on either side, I caught that sickening scent coming in at the window and saw the one in the passenger seat nodding and the edge of his smile when he turned to the driver and poked him in the shoulder.

"Jimmy," he said. "Do you smell anything?"

"No," Jimmy said.

They seemed to materialize out of the roadside growth itself, and they were as twisted and wound together as the vines and tendrils they hacked at with axes and machetes that flashed occasionally in the dull light filtering through the canopy that hung over them. I counted twenty dark figures and two pale ones and saw the heavy pile of chain in the road's center as the car slowed and stopped. They seemed to have no shoulders, their thin willowy arms growing out from the sides of their necks. All were bare to the waist, and their stomachs protruded, rounded below their sunken chests, as if they were starved, pregnant women. One paused and looked over from his work, his eyes set deep in their bony sockets. I heard a snarl from the far side of the car, and saw him look away and start in again at the hacking. When I turned I saw the sweaty face of the guard, his grin as he glanced in my direction, then leaned down on the sill and spoke into the open window up front.

"Here come the solution," he said.

"Jimmy, did'ya hear what he said?"

"Yeah," Jimmy said. "I heard'm."

The guard lingered at the car's side for no apparent reason than the passing of vacuous banter between himself and the man who sat in front of me. They jawed for a while, until I saw the driver look at his watch, grunt and engage the gearshift. We moved away then, and after a turning I could see where the road ended, the canopy of trees and the high chain-link gate, like the architecture of some official entrance into another world, and for some the only one.

I was wearing bush clothing I'd acquired in Argentina, a tan canvas shirt festooned with numerous buttoned pockets at the breast and arms, epaulets at the shoulders, and pants like riding breaches, leather leggings rising from my ankles to my knees, and a pith helmet I'd outfitted with beekeeper netting that I could roll down to cover my head and shoulders against mosquitoes and other stinging insects should I have occasion to enter swampland. I knew I looked striking, but when I stepped from the car and saw the castle walls, I thought some extravagant medieval wear would surely have been more appropriate.

We were a good seventy yards from the massive stone mansion, and it was clear they'd stopped there to give me the long, impressive view of things. Jimmy stayed in the driver's seat, shaded from the hot sun, but the other got out and ambled to the dusty front fender, where he proceeded to dig at his teeth with a metal instrument that seemed too large for the task. I stood at the door behind him, but could see clearly over his shoulder to where the truck, a flatbed with low wooden rails, was parked near a large steel slab set in the castle's outer wall.

I heard a creak and the grind of metal and the slippage of heavy links, then saw the huge slab opening like a drawbridge in the castle's side. It was lowered slowly until its edge was no more than a foot above ground. Then it fell, thudding into impacted earth, and billows of dust rose to obscure the view. There were muffled groans and snarls then in the distance, the slap of leather, and what I took to be light footsteps, shuffling in the click and rattle of chains.

They came as apparitions through the clouds of dust, their dark faces powdered by it, trails of sweat carving out masks reminiscent of those *kabuki* visages I'd seen in Tokyo, their arms like thin tree limbs half-flayed of bark. They were chained together on short tethers at wrists and ankles, bright silver chains, and they could not stride out, though guards to either side were urging them, herding them, their whips cracking indiscriminately, cutting into worn fabric at thighs and hips, and the men huddled together in mechanical necessity, lurching and stumbling in their slow and awkward progress, their feet shuffling on the wood and metal. Beyond desperation, somnambulistic, heads lifted skyward on their twisted necks, sun-blinded, mouths opening into dark empty holes, then closing without sound. The only change in sound came when the tortured music of the chains' rattle and scrape dulled as they left the bridge and were moving toward the truck bed, their feet in the dirt.

The man at the fender turned, still prodding at his teeth and sucking them, then lowered the tool to his side and spat into the dust at his feet. "Ten o'clock shift," he said. He may have been smiling, but I was not watching him. I was looking over his shoulder to where the men were struggling to climb up on the truck bed, the guards still beating them, the last few pulled up by others as the truck's engine coughed into life and it moved away, heading for us, then beyond us, leaving a whiff of that scent of decaying flesh I had smelled earlier, and where it had been, obscuring the view, I could now see the posts and their rusted chains and metal cuffs and the elevated wooden rack structure behind them where the figure lay, as if in ancient funereal order, a suicide I was to learn shortly, and on display, his body drained of its fat and the juice of organs, no more than a thin leather sack baking in the sun.

We crossed the drawbridge on foot and entered into the main prison yard, a space no more than a half-acre in size, at one time a courtyard or formal garden I thought, and rendered claustrophobic by the curving stone wall that climbed to a good seventy feet behind us. It was damp there, but cooler under the wall's shadows, and moss grew in the cracks where the stone slabs joined, forming geometric figures that rose to the wall's top, where metal spikes and sharp glass shards had been installed in the renovation.

Across the hard packed dirt in front of us, there was a wooden boardwalk fronting the castle's main entranceway, permanently sealed now, and to the sides of that were offices with names burned into wooden signs above their doors—*Guards, Procurator, Medical*—the largest holding the name *Warden*. I'd started off toward that one when the man called out to me, "Not yet." I turned and saw his sweaty face and the motion of his arm. He picked up my two heavy satchels, my leather briefcase under his arm, and I followed him toward the shadow of an archway off to the left where the building joined the curved outer wall, then through it and up a narrow stone stairway that turned back on itself several times before we reached a tight rectangular landing, a heavy wooden door at the end. The man dropped the suitcases, huffing, and yanked his soiled handkerchief from his pocket and mopped his brow. "Heavy," he said, as if to no one. I'd removed my pith helmet. It now hung from my fingers along my leg. He motioned again, toward the door this time, and once I'd passed him and had reached it and was pushing it open, I heard his soles squeaking as he descended the narrow passage.

The room was cool and oddly cheery given the previous circumstances, ones that I'd not organized in my brain just yet. Its walls were stone, even the one that separated off the large bathroom, and I was sure there had been no partitioning in the renovation here. Most probably it had been a guest room when the viscount was in residence. By the look of the bathroom, with its sunken tub, gold fixtures in the shapes of dolphins and sea nymphs, and the frieze above it, depicting a narrative of satyrs in pursuit of nubile virgins, I imagined it as a place for questionable dignitaries or concubines. There was an odd stone seat, a chair carved out of the material of the floor itself, just inches from the toilet bowl at eye level and facing it, and I could imagine what kind of decadence had been practiced there.

The room beyond was more conventional, though the bowl of fresh fruit, the whiskey bottle and ice bucket that were placed beside the folder on the low glass table, my name prominent on the cover in a fine cursive, suggested some academic convention rather than the prison consultation I'd come there for. The double bed seemed comfortable, under cover of its white spread, and as I reached for the folder I noted the chintz curtains, their wave in a humid breeze at the deep, stone windows, then read the brief letter topping the few documents.

It was from the warden. He was sorry, his schedule, the train problem, et cetera. He'd set up a meeting for the following day at noon. The important staff would be there. In the meantime, a man would come to my room at two p.m. I had free-range of the prison, and he would be my guide. He was the prison procurator, Hans Bonnefoy, grandson of the viscount himself, though son of a bastard child I was to learn later. I put the papers aside, then rose and went to the opulent bathroom, where I stripped away the bush outfit and washed and brushed my teeth. Then I returned and opened the suitcases, one on a rack provided, the other on the floor beside it. I selected a navy blue linen shirt, grey twill trousers, and my alligator belt and wingtips, then lay the clothing out neatly. I placed the diamond stud beside the wristwatch on the coffee table. It was eleven a.m. I had three hours to wait. So I lay back on the coverlet in my underwear and considered Bonnefoy, a procurator, and what use the prison might have for a position such as that. I had an idea already of how escape was possible, and I considered that for a while. Then I drifted into a light and awkward sleep, troubled by images of dusty figures and the scent of fruit and decay.

✦SEVEN✦

"To promote this history of the troubled South and to forestall reformation."

The words were spoken as if read from some brochure, and
their echo was light and confused among the massive stone pillars
supporting the castle floor. I'd asked that he take me to the basement first, this Hans Bonnefoy who had knocked softly at the wood-
en door of my room precisely at two p.m. He was a thin and dapper
man in his early fifties, small and with just a few wisps of hair above
his ears. His clothing hinted of the military, a tight brown suit with
a row of tarnished brass buttons rising almost to his throat.

"And because I needed the job," he said, a touch of irony in
his rheumy eyes. I wondered if he too was syphilitic, like his grandfather and maybe his father as well, though not yet mad.

The viscount had never married, but had sired many bastards, some like Bonnefoy's father with Cajun women, and all had come to the castle at his bidding and for the money and goods available there. He'd come with his father when he was just a child and had seen many of the others, their awkward, palsied movement and erratic behavior. He had stolen away from them on any opportunity and had roamed the castle's confusion of rooms and alcoves, had walked the battlements, explored even the massive basement where we now stood. He knew the place, both before and after renovation, and this is why the warden had assigned him as my guide. His position as procurator had been his cooptation. As a grandson, though illegitimate, he'd had actions lingering in the courts for many years. The warden had hired him, offering a sound and lucrative contract, and he had signed the paper disavowing his claims. He was a freelance agent, like I, but legally bound. He presented the prison's face as valuable history, himself as a tangible part of it, to that influential public the reformers had hopes to stir into action against it.

"Were you here when the kid escaped?" I asked.

"Oh, yes. Yes, indeed. That's what started it all, this constant stream."

"And they can't figure how it happens. And because of that they figure it must be one way only, and that's the frustration."

"Exactly right," he said.

"So they beat them, and some commit suicide in their despair."

That made him nervous, the implication of his part in it. He turned from our conversation and led me through the partitioned spaces until we came to the outer wall, where he tapped his fingernail against the dank stone.

"When I was a child," he said, "there was nothing much down here, only the pillars and these walls. Oh, the wine cellar was, but they tore that out, and there were a few rooms my grandfather kept private. Even now there are metal cuffs cemented in there, remnants, you know? But they're all storage rooms now, tools and repair materials. These outer walls are thick. They go down deep in the earth. Here, there is no way out."

The walls and floor were indeed impenetrable. Even were they not they'd provide nothing of significance, given that large open clearing and the high metal fence beyond it. Still, I asked Bonnefoy to guide me through the entire space, each irregular room and alcove. It was nearing four o'clock by the time I was satisfied. We left the basement then, making our way back to the floor above, where there were offices, the infirmary and mess hall, and a number of rooms sealed off with cemented cinder blocks filling their doorways. There were newly cemented walls blocking off hallways as well, and I was wondering if there was a pattern, something sealed away beyond, when we came to a solid steel door where Bonnefoy paused, tapping the metal as he had the outer wall.

"To the cells above," he said.

Time was getting on now, and I thought to leave the office floor for a later, complete examination, so I asked Bonnefoy to open the door and take me to where the prisoners were housed.

We entered into a narrow stone passage, rank with a scented stew of excrement, urine, and stale sweat. It was clammy there and dark, and our bodies cast fragmented shadows under dim bulbs high in the arched ceiling. I could smell blood too, neither fresh nor rancid, but refined in its ripening, like antebellum port.

"Is the sun still shining, do you think?"

There were gouged irregularities in the shadowed walls to either side, some seemingly fresh, bright cuts in the years of accretion. Bonnefoy was ahead, and when he spoke his voice was in a deep and muffled echo.

"The sun? There's no sun here."

But there was more dim light, a row of bulbs in metal cages as we reached the passage ending and began our ascent up the worn stone steps of a curving stairway, so tight I felt my elbows brushing the walls. I counted four complete turnings, though the tilt and curve of the passage was disorienting and I couldn't be sure of that number. Then we came to a small landing, a slab of metal at the end of it. I heard the click of Bonnefoy's keys as he unlocked the door, then followed him beyond that portal.

We were standing in yet another passage, but this one was wider, the stone across from us distinct under slightly brighter light and, though grimy, unscarred. A wash of bluish light spilled over the floor to our left and Bonnefoy headed that way, to where a thick glass window looked out across the passage to a metal gate. Behind the window was an office, four uniformed guards sitting in swivel chairs, two with their feet up on the wooden desk. One glanced at the diamond in my lobe as we came into view, then looked quickly away. Another rose and headed lazily for the door beside the rectangular window when Bonnefoy gestured. He was fat and unkempt, a flap of his shirt untucked and waving over his crotch when he emerged, and I caught Bonnefoy's eye, the two of us in our carefully arranged clothing, as if we were passing judgment on the gauche at some cocktail party in a civil world.

The man held a single large key on a metal ring. A skeleton key, I thought, almost nothing. Then the gate swung open quietly and we stepped into sound more subdued than in any other prison I'd visited, a dull modulated moaning, punctuated only by occasional coughs and wheezing, all muffled behind steel doors. The doors were not in rows, but appeared around turnings, back in dark alcoves, under archways where icons might have once rested. Some stood beside each other in places where the castle's rooms had been divided, but for the most part they came into view singly as we wound our way through passages and down sets of brief stairs. The scents that had permeated that passage where we'd ascended were here too, but altering in prominence as we moved past various doors and came into airless cul-de-sacs. Our passage seemed endless.

Bonnefoy was gracious in the way he kept looking back at me, expectant, moving to the side to allow my view into cells through the small rectangular slits cut into the doors at eye level, which was almost useless, dark as it was there. I could see shadows, a curve of wall, what may have been human figures but appeared only as piles of rags. Then we came to a cell that was set at the castle's perimeter, and I asked if we might enter there. Bonnefoy moved immediately to the door and inserted the key.

"Careful," I said. "Shouldn't you be careful?"

"Not to worry," he said, and pushed the door open to its fullest extent.

The back wall of the cell was the castle's outer wall, a dramatic curve making it clear it had been fashioned into one of the many turrets. There was a window-like opening there, a narrow tunnel that extended for a good five feet before reaching the outer air. Late afternoon light entered, but produced only a gray glow, just enough to distinguish the shape of the room, to see the slop and water buckets and the figure on the narrow cot off in the corner. He lay on his back, arms folded across his chest, and I had to watch for a while before I saw his hands rise slightly in his shallow breathing. Bonnefoy stayed near the doorway as I examined the cell, satisfying myself of what I'd expected in a few moments. Shadows played on the walls, slowly shifting. Then I heard something, a whispered croak, and when I turned to the man stretched out in his ragged prison garments, I saw his fingers moving slowly across his chest.

I stepped to the cot and sat down at the edge near the man's narrow hips. He was a black man, his color washed away into a powdery greyness in his sunken cheeks and along the ridge of his protruding nose.

"Are you ill?" I whispered, my face just inches from his own. I could smell his breath, clarified through long exhaustion into a light sweetness.

"Just tired," he said. "Tired, Jesse. Is it time?"

"No," I said. "Not now. But pretty soon."

"Well, I'm ready I guess. Can you do it quick? Just the one cut. I'll be sleeping, maybe."

"Okay," I said. "But you can rest now. It will be a while. Go back to sleep."

I awoke at one in the morning, having readied myself before going to bed. Bonnefoy had brought a dinner to my room, disappointed that I'd opted for an early night and to eat alone, and I'd agreed to a late breakfast at his office before the warden's meeting at noon. The dinner consisted of pork ribs, their juice leaking into greasy mashed potatoes. But there were at least vegetables, and once I'd plucked the mushy okra from the stew, I'd found the over-cooked peppers and cucumbers at least edible. The beer was cool enough. Bonnefoy had noted pointedly that the cooking was not his.

Standing in the bathroom, I thought of the man in his cell. It was merciful murder he'd anticipated, but a fake suicide, a diversion I was sure for Jesse's planned escape. I wondered how many suicides had been faked ones and thought not many, a ploy that would too soon become obvious pattern.

When I returned to the other room, I gathered my stud, together with my watch and rings rolled up in a sock, and tucked the soft packet into my suitcase. Then I dressed again in my bush clothing, all but the boots, and pulled on the soft black slippers. There was starlight at the window, blinking through drifting cloud cover, but no moon. Shadows played on the dark walls. The circumstances were perfect, and I left the room, my toes pressing the stone as if I were barefoot, and headed across the landing and down the narrow passage to the castle's first floor.

I was quite apparent in my bush clothing, the jodhpurs, those tight leggings and the shirt of numerous pockets and epaulets, under one of which I'd tucked the black gloves as an echo of the slippers, which appeared ludicrous, in no way part of my costume. When I confronted the first figure that appeared, a guard with swollen cheeks and lips who looked Neanderthal and half-asleep in his stooped posture, he eyed me up and down, then proclaimed that I must be the consultant, but with a question mark at the end of his statement.

"Isn't it obvious?" I said. He grunted, neither in assent nor recognition of the humor, and I showed him the warden's letter. I'd underlined the passage giving me complete access. I followed behind his stooped and bowlegged figure, heading for the heavy metal door, which he unlocked, then stood aside to allow my passage. I heard the door thud shut behind me as I moved lightly into the powerfully smelling chamber once again, then came to the curving stairway and headed up. When I reached the second door, I proceeded to bang on it with my fist. After a few moments it was opened by another guard, who checked my papers with more careful attention, then took me to the gate across from the office window, unlocked it, and let me in. I could feel his eyes on my back as I moved down the passage, came quickly to the first turning, then headed directly to the cell where Bonnefoy had taken me earlier and inserted the key I'd lifted from his ring when he'd brought dinner to my room. The cell was much darker than it had been before, yet a faint starshine entered at the tunnel window. I could see the bed, the slop and water pails beside it and the metal tray on the floor near its foot, lumps of uneaten food vibrating slightly in the roiling of some vermin reducing it. The man was still in the bed, and I moved across the floor to him, then bent over near his face to find breath that was shallow but almost regular. Delirium or sleep, I couldn't tell. I stood beside him, then pulled forth the thin black garments secreted below my bush shirt and laid out the *shinobi shozoku* across the man's wasted body in preparation for dressing.

It was in Tokyo where I'd learned the ancient practice of *ninjutsu* and the art of the shadow warriors. I was trained by an old man whose name I can't reveal. I'd been there on vacation during turbulent times. War with China was pending, and even the prison system, known for its severity and order, was edging into disarray. I'd visited a few, as a tourist, but had soon let it be known that I was somewhat knowledgeable and had gotten access to the inner workings. I'd been at one prison when a man, my eventual teacher, had been released with a group of others after many years of incarceration for vague crimes that seemed purely political, though I was to learn later, much to my great chagrin, that they were entirely other than that.

There'd been a private celebration near the inner gates, and by happenstance I was there among the authorities who stood silently by as the prisoners greeted relatives in a courtyard beside a placid lily pond at the edge of a stone garden. The man caught my eye, and moved by the occasion I called out a few phrases in Japanese from my meager store. They contained the words Freedom and Justice, and I spoke them stridently.

Needless to say, the authorities I stood among were not pleased by my outburst, but the man had smiled and bowed in my direction. And later, again coincidence, I saw and approached him when I was strolling through a park in the crowded city.

The man had been a *genin* or field agent for one of the last ninja *ryus* active in Japan in the third quarter of the previous century. His organization had hired out its skills in infiltration and assassination and was working for organized crime at the time he was caught and incarcerated. He was eighty-five years old, but fit and alert, though he had spent more than half his life in prison. And he was in need of money.

I gave up tourism, paid him his meager fee, and though I'd planned to be in Tokyo for three weeks only, I stayed there for two months. The instruction was intense, most of it having to do with the ninja arts of invisibility and misdirection. I'd learned the basics, just enough to realize I knew almost nothing at all. Still I'd practiced these skills on my Wisconsin acreage, stalking rabbits and even deer. Once I was able to stand at the shoulder of a grazing buck.

I dressed slowly and carefully, lifting each garment in turn and slipping it over my bush clothing, which was an awkwardness but a necessity, and when the loose shirt and trousers were in place, I applied the burnt cork to my already swarthy face. I'd brought the cork from Wisconsin, had packed it with the ninja gear, and I had noted its name earlier when I was scorching it near the window in my room. It was the one Danker had pulled from that fine bottle of Condrieu only days before. Then I adjusted the wrap at my forehead, under the soft mobile hood reminiscent of nuns of certain orders. The veil hung loose at my breast. I attached it to cover my face and neck, then pulled the black gloves over my fingers.

The figure on the bed was freed of my garments now and seemed to breathe more easily as if they'd been an oppressive weight. Looking up from his body I measured a soft-edged shadow on the curving outer wall, then lifted an arm and shoulder and drifted away from the bed in imitation of it. I couldn't see myself, of course, but could note a partial melding in my dissembling movements, a trick of invisibility designed to cast the watcher's eyes in a wrong direction. The strictures of the bush clothing rendered movement awkward, far from my intended grace, though good enough for here I hoped, among these dull attentions. Shadows were general in the prison, a characteristic so obvious it had gone unnoticed for the part it might play in escape, but I was familiar with roles of the obvious and had taken careful note of them, even those in bright sun and dust, when I'd been privy to that theatrical progress of the chain gang prisoners in my first moments in view of the castle.

As I attempted the narrative of another move, I heard the bell begin its sounding, a series of deep percussive bongs, each stroke following upon a pause that ended only as the previous one faded, as if some sweaty and bare-chested figure in a turban were striking the occasion laboriously with a two-handed mallet.

"Jesse?" A whisper only under the worn fabric of his clothing as I turned and headed for the door, hearing the dull shuffle and clank of chains even before I opened it. I stepped out into the dim passageway; then, hugging into the walls' shadows, I drifted ahead in my split-toed *tabi* until I reached the final turning, where I paused and squatted down on my haunches. I shook my head to loosen the shapeless cap and peeked around at the edge to see guards with their whips in half-darkness and others, squatting as I was, but in brighter light, attaching the ankle chains to the row of stoop-shouldered figures.

I saw a movement in shadow at the far wall where the guards with the whips were standing, some light playing down the passage from a stone window opening, altering as clouds flowed over stars to cause changes in density and an expansion into fuzziness at the shadow's edges. Before that movement and undulation was lost to me, I rose and stepped back a few feet, then raised my arms and knee to flutter and shift my garments so that they no longer outlined a human figure, but were like drapery or windblown clothing on a line. I moved out slowly into the passage then, stepping in

jerky movements to keep my black garments drifting. The guards
had risen from the prisoners' feet now and were working the chains
into rings at their wrists. They seemed too close to the prisoners,
almost pressing into them. A few were grunting in their work and
the mild frustration of that task and its needful coordination. The
long chain was being pulled through, taut and then slack, and the
guards called sharp commands to each other and to the prisoners
as well. The guards at the wall were watching, taking pleasure in
the sweaty labor of others. My passage was only a few feet and the
desire to move quickly was heavy upon me, but I fought it, kept
concentration on grace and shape, knowing that a glance might
catch me unless I was the never-seen-before, and thus attributed to
a trick of light. When I reached the wall, I pressed into it, joining
my constructed figure to that of the shadow there, then undulated
also, in rhythm with its changes.

Now the guards with the whips had stepped forward from
the shadows beside mine and were moving along the row of prisoners, thirty or more gaunt souls, searching them roughly and
without care for any privacy. I saw hands grope at groins, fingers
poking deep into mouths and ears. One was slow in compliance,
and the guard struck him half-heartedly, as might a betrayed and
despairing lover. I could see down the diminishing hallway to the
metal door, and when I altered my head device and turned within
it, I saw the shifting light at the stone window. I was keeping its
rhythm, my gloves slipping back and forth in the changing geometry. Then I saw into the shadow cast on the wall a few feet away,
separated from my own by a hazy square of light entering from
the passage mouth where I too had entered. It moved also, but less
convincingly.

"Jesse," I whispered.

His response came from deep wondering. I could hear the
fight for control in it.

"Who you?"

"Pollard," I said. "Friend of the kid."

"The kid?" he said. "The kid long gone."

"Like this," I said. "Quiet now. Follow me."

There was a dull clang as the metal door was opened, then clicks and ripples when the dark figures turned in its echo, their chains slipping at ankles and through the steel rings at their wrists. I took the opportunity in that quiet cacophony and stepped away from the wall, trusting that Jesse was behind me, and followed the back of the last guard, then heard a distinctly different sound, some foreign pebble stowaway, or a bit of brittle twig brought up from the roadway in the tread of a rubber shoe, Jesse's slipper kicking or sliding over it. The guard ahead paused. I could see his ears perk, and as he turned I raised my arms to block off Jesse's figure behind me and formed the shadow image of a windblown tree, impossible in reality there at mid-passage, but convincing. I'd dusted my lids and long lashes with the burnt cork, and I steadied my eyes, flecks of light in acorns. The guard peered, not at me but into me, to see through to the stone window where the wind must be, then blinked and gave it up and turned again, and I with Jesse trailing hovered close behind him until he reached the prisoners who were now no longer in a regimented line, but had become a ragged crowd at the metal doorway opening into darkness. We slipped by him then and pressed in among the others, some of whom grunted knowingly at our intrusion, and melded into their ragged garment folds and the overlapping complex of shadows cast by moving limbs and torsos.

How, then, describe the qualities of our tortuous descent, that twisted narrow passage and its scents glutted with our humanity? Guards were in the front and some behind, pushing back and urging on, though keeping their distance. One had raised a handkerchief to cover his mouth and nose. I was folded among bodies, embracing them, at times carried in the malleable crush. "Jesse?"

A whisper. "Who the fuck you?" But no matter. We were a tide. I felt hands at my breast, the negotiation of a leg slipping between my own, fingers at my hip. A chorus of moans, some bodies lifted like mine, the lame and exhausted, scents of decay in breath and dried human waste moistened back into vibrancy in fresh sweat, a communal stew, evidence of that slow fade back to the earth, but still alive, the stumbling and inert, all forced to mobility, yet free in our sophisticated handling of the limbs and parts of others, an austere and social accommodation. There was dim light at the ending, and we spilled out into the passage and saw the whips unfurl. Then we entered into the high-walled courtyard, a few stars in the sky above, and felt a light humid breeze as the drawbridge lowered and the whipping began, brutal and mechanical, without rage or apparent motivation.

Jesse was ahead now, stumbling in the common stupor and quite apparent, but it made no difference. The shadows were numerous and without pattern. The truck cast its own, still and rectangular, and the rack's was a skeletal figure. I felt a whip cut into my calf, heard the snap, then pressed in among the others with a guilty feeling, avoiding further assault. Then I felt my feet leave the bridge and hit solid ground, and I moved among bodies to get to Jesse.

The men were climbing over the truck's lowered gate now, urged on by the whips and the commands of those without whips, and I took Jesse's arm and pushed him ahead to the truck's side. All the guards were back with the last chained stragglers, those weaving and half-falling and those dragged. They were poking them with sticks, still whipping them, and I pushed Jesse into the truck's rear wheel, then passed him and reached to the flatbed for a purchase, finding metal hooks and rectangular holes used for stakes. When I glanced back I saw he had done the same. We hung there, our loose black garments rippling in the breeze as the engine coughed into life, gears ground, and the truck headed across the acre of open space toward the fence and the gnarled growth at the road opening. It moved slowly enough, even slower once it had entered at the mouth and was bouncing along the rough surface, and when the canopy of trees and vines was thick enough to blot out the sky and we were in a deep darkness, I released my grip and fell down at the turning tire, then rolled into the drainage ditch and felt the weight of Jesse's light body thud into my back, his fingers searching among the fabric at my armpit.

We lay there, listening to the truck's throbbing engine as the sound receded. Jesse remained collapsed on me, as if I were a bed much better than the one he'd taken fitful sleep in all those fifteen years.

"We take our turns," he told me.

We'd revived and had moved into deeper growth, well away from the road, and were sitting knee to knee, our backs against tree trunks.

"And what now?" I said. "You're not out of the woods yet."

He laughed lightly, his teeth bright in the darkness. He'd removed his black clothing to reveal himself as a farmhand in bib overalls, hand-made I could tell, but passable.

"They's others went before me, after the kid showed us. They'll be waiting. Just a long little walk."

"Won't they send dogs?"

"Well, they might," he said. "But shan't for eight hours at least. I'll be away by then."

I thought to ask him about the kid, for details, but didn't want to hold him there, so I helped him dig a hole and bury his escape costume, then gripped him tight in my arms and kissed him on the cheek.

"One other thing," I said, as he was turning to go. "The man in the cell, were you to kill him?"

"I was," he said. "But I couldn't."

He touched my hand, then stepped away among the tree trunks, and in moments I was stripping off my own dark garments and was spreading them over my breast under my bush shirt.

A guard accosted me when I reached the fence and road's mouth again and was stepping into starlight in view of the castle. He looked down at my leggings, recognizing who I was.

"Just reconnoitering," I said, and though it was clear he had no idea what the word meant, he turned his rifle barrel to wave me through. I heard his voice behind me as I headed for the drawbridge.

"Bleeding out your leg," he said. "Better get something on that."

→EIGHT←

The procurator's office was small, each surface piled high with papers, envelopes, and brochures with color renderings on their covers. Sun had not yet reached beyond the high stone wall. Lamps were lit, and once Hans Bonnefoy had called out in answer to my knock and I'd entered, I saw the dull glimmer at the small of his back where the suspenders crossed through a brass buckle.

"Rustling up our victuals!" he said brightly, turning to reveal himself in a flower print apron, the tails of his bow tie loose at the neck and a long fork in his hand.

"Sit down! Have a seat! There's coffee!"

I could smell the rich brew, hear the sizzle of potatoes frying. He'd carved out a neat place at the room's end, a small round table covered in a cheery check, white plates, silver, and crystal goblets, a few long stemmed roses in a delicate vase at the center.

"There's orange juice!" he said.

"Well, now," I said. "This is wonderful."

Bonnefoy cooked, his elbows dancing as he sliced onions and whisked eggs in a metal bowl. He wore white trousers, his suspender straps colorfully reminiscent of patterns in the Confederate flag, and his shirt was white too, his white jacket on a wooden hanger at a coat rack off in the corner, a broad-brimmed hat perched above it. I wondered if he had readied himself for the noon meeting and thought it was not likely. While he prepared the meal, I fingered through the papers on the desk where I sat, then picked up a brochure from a stack near the edge. Its cover pictured the welcoming entranceway to a large manor house in the Southern style, a broad veranda supported by wooden columns, leaded glass doors standing wide open above the graceful steps. I could see the edge of a bright carpet near the sill, and the windows were hung with airy silk curtains. The shaded porch held wicker chairs and tables, and a large rocker sat at an angle near the doors. I could almost hear the darkies singing. Printed below the rendering was the viscount's name and the indication that this was his home.

"Where *is* this place?" I asked.

Bonnefoy had finished up his work and had slid the omelets onto our plates beside the bowl of crisp fried potatoes and curls of translucent onion. He was arranging sprigs of parsley when I spoke. He held one in his fingertips and paused, a quizzical look upon his face, then waved it toward the wall.

"Why, *here*," he said. "Right here."

While I savored his delicious breakfast, Bonnefoy spoke of his central procurator duties, the dissemination of seductive information, such as the brochure, that would draw influential visitors to the viscount's palatial dwelling and its history, all right here at the castle's other side.

"It's another front against the threats," he said. "They really do see the place as an experiment in penology, which for them means good prisoners are passive ones. No escapes, of course. That's why you're here. They managed a good deal of support for the restoration, though of course it's a fake one."

"Do you have any antiseptic?" I asked. "Bandaging?" While he searched in a cabinet, I placed the cell key beside his ring on an empty chair.

The whip had cut deep, coming through the black fabric where my jodhpurs met the leggings, and though I'd dressed the wound in the early morning hours before sleep, I could feel a wetness and a slight throbbing. The pain was nothing troublesome, but I feared a leaking through the compress I'd applied, a staining of my twill trousers. They were dull grey in color, a flatness in the weave that pushed the tight patterning into subtle apparency. They complimented my charcoal linen shirt perfectly. Again I wore the alligator shoes and belt, and I'd inserted the diamond stud, couching it in a curl of hair that I'd affixed at my lobe with pomade.

I'd lowered my pants, and Bonnefoy had been gracious in kneeling at my feet and tending to me, swabbing the wound clean, then redressing it and wrapping my leg efficiently with gauze from knee to calf. It was ten-twenty by the time he was finished. The tour would begin at eleven, and once we'd enjoyed a last cup of coffee, he led me to the door and we made our way beyond the outer wall, then circled the castle to the far side. There was no access from within the building.

The sun was high now, but a light breeze was blowing from the right direction, and there was little unpleasant humidity. We strolled leisurely, cool in the shadows cast under the castle's stone walls, our conversation woven only of after-breakfast trivialities.

I left Bonnefoy standing at the viscount's French doors in his white suit and hat, his bow tie perky at his throat. The tour vehicles had arrived, two long limousines and a small bus, and I saw the ladies in their fine flowered dresses, parasols turning at their shoulders, coming down the broad stone walkway from the gate as I stepped from the porch and headed back to the darker side of the castle. The way was blocked by a metal gate set in a high stone wall covered with ivy, as if a garden were beyond. Bonnefoy had left the door ajar for me to close tight once I'd passed through. Then I was entering over the drawbridge again, heading for the warden's office and the orientation meeting, a useless exercise, for though I had been there for only a few hours, I'd already solved the puzzle of escape and had no intention at all of revealing my findings. This shocking conclusion came to me only as I lifted my hand to knock at the warden's door and with it the realization that I would be truly on the other side now, though I'd never given thought to sides. The seed had been planted only recently in Arizona and with the kid in Mexico. Mine had been a profession of dilemmas and the solving of them, mechanics and imagination, but I knew then that things would be changing.

We met in a room off a hallway behind the warden's office, a small amphitheater that I was sure had been a bath or sauna in the viscount's time. Broad marble steps rose from the tiled floor, and my foot found what I thought was a drain under the table, facing them as I sat down. I could imagine naked men and women sitting in steam, casks of water and dippers hanging from their sides, which the six unattractive figures I faced might have made use of, for they had come directly from work and sweat glistened on their foreheads and was evident in large dark stains flooding from their armpits. Pig-faced men, their brows vacant of subtlety, who dug in their crotches as dogs might, absently searching for fleas. One sat a little off from the others; he wore a black eye patch, a leather glove on one hand, and shifted occasionally, favoring a bad knee.

The warden stood at the table's side. He was fat also, but his tan uniform was dry and carefully pressed and he had cooled himself in a bath of bay rum, the dark, decaying scent of which had permeated the entire room even before we'd all settled and he'd coughed and made my introduction. "Mr. Pollard," he'd said. "The consultant."

And that was all he'd said, leaving the content of my orientation to me, something I'd experienced many times before. I was after all the interloper, there invariably in question of their competence. And then there was my look. The faces stared at me, my hair, the diamond stud, that fine shirt, and I displayed a half smile, ambiguously seductive, looking carefully at each in turn until he looked away, all but the one-eyed man, who held the intensity of my look, even through a hazy watering at his pupil. Once I'd articulated a time frame and the assistance I'd be needing, it was he who raised the kind of accusatory question I'd been expecting.

"Why don't we just keep beating them? Do it more."

"Why not," I said. "You could break their legs, their arms too. That might solve the problem."

"Can we do that?" one of the others said, and the one-eyed man scoffed at him.

"Did you know the kid?" I asked.

"Oh, yeah, the kid," another chimed in.

"No," I said. "I mean him."

I'd pointed to the one-eyed man. He snarled, slapping his knee.

"This. And this eye. And *this* too," he spat, lifting his gloved fist. The warden raised his own hand to calm him, and I had no heart for any more of it.

I told them I'd need a week, would be going into every cell, and that they'd find me in places they might not expect. The warden told them to answer any questions, to instruct all other guards as to my access. I said I'd be wearing the bush clothing I'd arrived in, that no one would mistake me, and the one-eyed man bit off a bitter laugh. There was room for me to needle him more extensively about the kid, but Bonnefoy's breakfast bile was rising in my throat, a profound distaste at my dissembling. I was already thinking ahead to the task of my report and its necessary falseness. I wanted out of there, to be home in Wisconsin. I wanted to be fishing.

⇢NINE⇠

Jesse's escape was discovered just an hour after our meeting ended and the suicide shortly after. The man had sawed open his own throat with a tin dinner plate, the edge of which had been rendered jagged through repeated scraping on the stone floor. There were maggots in the wound and bits of rotted food that only maggots would eat. He must have carved away in some painless delirium, for the cuts were multiple and rough, veins and arteries severed only after a good deal of steady work.

I was sleeping, having collapsed on the bed fully dressed, worn out after the late hours I'd kept, and the steady beat of the gong must have been sounding for a long time before I came awake, then staggered to the door where I could hear running feet and muffled voices below. I went to the bathroom and washed up, then descended the narrow stairway and headed for Bonnefoy's procurator office, keeping close to walls and moving quickly through doorways to avoid the languidly hysterical peregrinations of the guards who went this way and that, then returned to where they'd been and headed out again. Bonnefoy sat behind his desk drinking iced tea, a sprig of mint brushing his lips, well out of the fray.

"You've heard?" he asked, then told me about Jesse and the suicide. "A shame, and useless."

"So you know," I said, moving to a chair at the desk end. "Useless as diversion?"

"I've suspected, though not exactly how. They go out in the shift changes, don't they?"

"Yes," I said. "But you haven't mentioned your suspicions? Not to them, I mean."

He leaned back in his chair, chewing at the mint, his upper lip stained a light green.

"Them," he said. "Well, *I'm* not them. And I'm sick of all this."

"Me too," I said.

"And I'm going to do something about it. To hell with the contract, this depressing security."

"That's the ticket," I said. "I can't help you, but I won't help them. If I'm contacted, for some verification of conditions, then I will help. I'll report exactly what's going on here, what I've witnessed at least."

"That's good enough," he said.

He poured me a glass of tea then, and we spoke of other things, home and what it meant to him and what Wisconsin meant to me.

I finished the week under cover of my dissembling consultation, examining the cells, asking questions and taking notes.

The days dragged by, though interrupted pleasantly by occasional breakfast meetings with Bonnefoy, and when the time came for my departure I was deep in a blue funk that lasted through the entire drive back to Shreveport. Jimmy was at the wheel as before, his crude companion the same, but I engaged them in no repartee and only nodded as I left the car in front of the train station, where the funk began to lift as soon as they had driven away.

When I reached the compartment, I stripped and showered in the small stall, then dressed in my burgundy silk pajamas. Then it was night and the train was moving. I sat at the window looking out until I felt my lids falling, then crawled into the narrow bed and slept most of the way to Chicago. I was refreshed by the time I got there and saw Danker's welcoming smile under his new fedora.

My report was empty of all vilification and was written to the chirp of sparrows and the first fall warblers nesting in pines near my cabin window. It would be my last report, for a while at least. Upon returning, I'd found nothing in the mail waiting. There was another job, still pending near Caracas, and one in New York City, but they were many months away and still uncertain, and I vowed to accept no others in the interim.

I penned in my signature, then watched the ink dry. The report had been nonsense, ending with a review of possible escape routes and comments about the need for better guard training and tighter schedules. What I'd written was the truth, but for that crucial omission, and yet none of the suggested alterations would make any significant difference. Their brutality had been effective, a depressive draining of any sufficient energy for action, and it had taken the kid, as it had in Arizona, to raise hope again.

As the birds nested, so did the weary travelers, those jet-tisoned from larger mass movements to set out toward winter in an unfriendly north. I couldn't help thinking of them in terms of the brutality near Shreveport. Here, America was the prison, its borders the walls with no hope within them, and yet the prisoners kept moving, albeit thrust forward in desperation. These conceits, the cycle of nature and the romance of incarceration, both were indulgence. I'd seen ice along the lake's shore, a child in rags at the ice shack door. A few were ensconced in a broken down tractor shed far from any other structure. I'd come across their traps and trout lines, set with care, but without sufficient knowledge of local behaviors. We'd put out stale bread crumbs for the birds, but nothing much for them, though Danker had hired a few to clear brush and fallen tree limbs from the long road in and to help Count Southpaw with the yearly mulching. They were gaunt men and women, their children huddled on stumps, watching in the fall sun. Now we were considering a schedule for a thorough cleaning and repair of the stables and were again discussing the opening of the old servants' quarters when winter came on in earnest.

Still, the birds were singing, it was warm in the cozy cabin, and late afternoon light lifted the red and yellow flowers of the portulaca in my window box, their petals rising up from a light dusting of snow. Then the phone rang, our private line between house and cabin. It was Danker, and it was Avery Brattle again. This time he was taking no excuses and was coming over.

"Okay," I said. "Give him a drink or something. I'll be down in a half-hour."

I selected a fall outfit, a slightly severe gray jacket worn over a burgundy blouse and a matching skirt, and I stuffed my meerschaum down in the pocket for later. My stockings were flannel and without pattern, opaque enough to cover the thin gauze bandaging below my knee. When I tilted the vanity mirror I saw that my cheeks were rosy enough and needed no makeup. Then I combed my short hair, bringing the front down into bangs, the sides to a pageboy at my ears. I stood up then and turned and smoothed my skirt over my narrow hips and checked the hem. I was ready enough for Avery Brattle, and I left through the cabin's front door and started down the broad, snow dusted trail in my practical low heels.

There are those I believe who recognized me as a woman but couldn't come to acknowledge what their eyes were telling them. I played the clichés, with my clothing and the choice of it in regard to tastefulness, and most of all with the diamond stud and the way I dressed it with a curl, things they could only conceive of as female. But I was accomplished, more than they in their world, and they thought of women as having no real intelligence at all and thus couldn't make the short step, from recognition to belief and revelation.

It was not the sex talk and its crude brutality and childishness, but the harder judgment against women and their essential stupidity that blinded them. With the gaucho shirt and then the Louisiana bush clothing, I'd carried things a bit far, not into risk but a kind of decadent indulgence. I could have worn a harlequin's outfit after all and gotten away with it. I played them like the primitive instruments they were, plucking their dull imaginations gonadotropically, for that was after all where they were seated.

They couldn't think of women as ignorant, not in the face of so many informed skills that accused their own abilities, things they knew they couldn't do half as well. The simple art of cooking, grace in shopping and keeping an orderly family, the complexities of house management and budgetary juggling. But the foolishness of stupidity was another matter, one that could not be squared with the inventiveness and competence they were forced to acknowledge in me. They were confused in their own gender too and made a mirror of me, one they clouded with half-conceived images to keep the threat in me at a proper distance. Fairy, whore, shape-shifter, powerful exotic, magician, dandy, or artist, all these and much more. They couldn't really see me, here in nineteen-thirty-five, and I could pass easily among them in practice of my profession, something that would have been impossible had I announced myself as Christine Pollard.

I'm the same person. I love fishing and hunting, cold and warm weather on my skin, travel and the complexities of human exchange. I'm fond of clothing, good food, and very good wine. I'm athletic, but I don't like dancing, beating around the bush, the humorless, or that stupid bestiality in the vacuously self-righteous. And I love my work too, even in its commerce among such men, though I would not dress in a parody of their clothing to practice it were that possible.

The work: consultation and calculation, imagination, the powers of the mind realized in solution.

It's as a woman that I need and want this profession, one that didn't even exist before I invented it, though its ethics have become clearly questionable in recent weeks. But then I've had a different point of view, even as I grow tired of it all and look ahead now beyond Avery Brattle to the frozen lake and my line in the luminous blue hole.

→TEN←

Buck took a place in sun at the schoolhouse wall where he could grovel somewhat and whine for his benefit and was soon coveted. Winter was in that land, a chill breeze and ice in crystals in his matted fur that he could lick away for the cold comfort of sustenance, and when the sun went down he was often discomfited in the lee of grease-spattered snow drifts among rusted metal kitchen appliances that, in cover of dark night, were rifled by tattered figures who carried off what little they could manage, utilitarian objects from which could be made cook stoves and shallow, leaking pots.

People lived in the woods now and stood to the sides of sagging, patched tents near the river, pounding the metal with dull energy in their listless, boredom-relieving fashion. All along the river, low fires in the night, and in the woods too, and when the woods were full, men would come with lanterns to drive them away, whole families, at times with hogs and chickens, seldom with the indulgence of dogs, and to speak against them as they were gathering their meager belongings.

In the day they moved along the dirt roads in packs, as Buck had, but more slowly, unrelated or only half of them related, others taken in or driven off by the tattered figures themselves, whose clothing absorbed the winter sun, nothing anymore about their bodies to reflect it, but for an occasional ring band, dull on a woman's finger. They moved, more circuitously, through fields of fallow crops, bending at times for their rooting, or to simply lie there like cast away bundles among the frozen stalks.

Buck had eaten cold and bitter corn as they had and he'd eaten a snake. Once he'd eaten bits of rotting flesh that he could not identify, even after his grass emetic and the disgorgement, when he'd nosed among the gobbets of that hot stew, before eating that too. He tried for fresh kill, but he was slow now and weary, and there was little available; the few chickens left in cages were guarded, as were the meager pickings among the other livestock. There were gardens, but little in them; the potatoes had rotted, the ground frozen now above them. He'd chewed bits of bark left by deer and fallen winter apples.

The people were falling down into the land, just as Buck was, and trying to eat it, but always others had been there before them and had devoured it. There was nothing left, almost nothing, and there was nothing to do but to be moving, like these children who were moving by him on their way home from school, some in passable clothing, others to continue on, who would not be returning. A few dropped bits of lint-speckled food from their pockets in response to his whining, not enough but something, and this is why he took up station there at the building's edge, his head in cold breeze, but in sun, his body guarded in shadow from the wind.

Buck trailed behind her small figure, limping in wheel ruts in the blasted road. She had turned to him and now she turned to make sure of his following. The road was empty of traffic but was scarred by it, and there were places where wagon and car wheels had gouged away the shoulder, beyond which stalks rose from conical dirt mounds in the pocked fields and fires burned in dusty twilight at horizon. There were useless leavings in the road's ruts and along the embankments, the abandoned past that followed domesticity's last abandonment, shards of home's broken appliances, tools, not of trade, but idiosyncratic house repairs, the romance of leisure left in ruined and rusted toys, angular adult board games, and the counted-on future in shattered canning jars, a few necks still screwed tight with their metal rings.

All wished only to be treated with some neutral attention, to be looked at without aggression or wariness, and though when they reached the barn, the door racked on its hinges and half open, the girl stood back a little from him, the gesture of her hand was unstinting as she urged him in. The shuttered house, the wagon piled high and tilting under its load at the porch steps as he passed through to find only straw leavings and the dirt floor patterned in dull light lines cast through separations at the barn board seams. He scratched the straw into a low pile and circled instinctively, then lay down there and went to sleep.

He awakened once in the night. The floor to his side was dark, but he saw the dim figure of the mouse moving across it, listlessly wending. He was on his side, the mouse at his level, or he was at its level. It moved close to his paw in the dirt, just inches away. He was not waiting, nor did he reach out for it. He was not laying in wait, stalking, nor did his hunger have the force of an energy in it. He turned his paw to the side, creating a concave wall, and soon the mouse moved into the lee of that furry shelter and the wall fell upon it. He heard nothing come from it as he crushed it, then slid his paw to his mouth. He chewed the mouse with delicacy, as one might the sacrament, and could distinguish its figure still on his tongue as he fell into sleep once again, only to be awakened at first light under the shadow of a thin man who was nudging him with his foot. He rose, awkward and shaking, then followed the man's pointed finger, moving to the barn door and out into the cold morning. A light snow was falling, had already dusted the loaded wagon and the figures who sat huddled together among the furniture there. "Git, now," the man said softly, and Buck headed off into the fields, half-blinded in the slanting snow.

He came up out of a root cellar set in the hillside at the orchard's end. It was still winter, and the apple trees were skeleton structures, vividly brittle against the slate sky. He lifted his leg and pissed a steaming flow, yellow and flecked with red crystals that pocked the crust of dirty snow at the tree's base and remained there as the urine sank away. Then he vomited up a half-digested mouse, one of the many bewildered ones that had come to him in the cellar's darkness looking for food and warmth. He'd eaten them and the few remaining edible roots. He'd eaten snow from the cleaner drifts for his liquid sustenance. It was bitter cold and his fur was filthy and woven into a wire-like matting that let the cold in against the scabs running along his flanks. The itch in them was gone away now, anesthetized under the matting's permanent frost.

After his escape from the prison of brutality and suicide, the kid and his dog headed north into the end of summer and the beginning of fall, arriving finally in a midwest state where the kid was taken once again, and for months Buck had been travel-ing deep into winter, alone and without purpose, other than the one that drew him to the progress of other travelers, those human ones he kept a good distance from, moving through woods and the ice-encrusted remnants of dead crops in open fields, following along with them wherever they might be headed, their heads down against the wind, shapeless in rags blowing in a listless dance around their bodies. At night he drew nearer to their fires, never close enough for warmth, and in the mornings, once they'd decamped, he searched in the cold embers and around them for bits of food, finding only meager scraps. Then he too would decamp and follow on to scent them in a while, then would move off again to flank them in their aimless journeying, himself in the same dull fix.

Now the sun broke through clouds at horizon and with it the sound of a flute over voices, and once he'd shuddered the last drops away he lowered his stiffened leg and limped back to the cellar where he slid down into the darkness, to a place where he could turn, then returned to the cellar's mouth to listen and keep watch. The voices were advancing, but then they gathered together into a punctuated murmuring. They were off, over the hill beyond the orchard's end, and after he'd listened to them for a while, scenting to be sure of them and their fixed location, he crawled out of the cellar again and into the bitter breeze that had come with the flute and the sun and made his way among the frozen trees until he was on his belly and edging up to the hill's barren crest where he could see down into their encampment; the automobile and trailer, their patched tents and the two iron cauldrons under which fires flickered in the coming twilight, and the pony.

There were seven of them, including the pony, and a small quick man, almost a dwarf, was looking up at a boy who held a ball under his arm. The man was dressed curiously in a long coat that had tails and he wore a tall hat. The boy was thin. They were talking. Then the boy turned and set off toward a barren hill beyond which the land was invisible, and the ball fell and rode down his arm to his hand, then fell to his foot. Then it came up high in the air and bounced on the boy's head, where it pinged, then fell to his hand again so that he could turn his hand over and bounce it before him on the ground. He caught it and tucked it under his arm as he reached the crest, stepped over it and disappeared.

There was a whinny then, the pony, and a plump little girl lifting the brushes. The pony had been covered in ragged blankets, but now its mane and tail were exposed to the air, bright blond and grey, those colors rendered more various in light flickers from the fires under the cauldrons near to which the girl had brought it for warmth and grooming. Her brushes were above her head now, moving along the pony's flanks, bringing up sheen. Drawn to this domesticity, the others were watching, the little man, and a man and a woman in heavy patchwork coats and gloves, their bodies ramrod straight, but hidden from definition under their weighty coverings. A man sat near a tent flap at a small table, working a deck of cards. Then the little girl was finished and had cast the blankets over the pony's back, and her hips swayed in her long, carpet-like skirt as she lifted a bucket from the ground and held it under the pony's muzzle so it could drink. The dwarf-like man had dipped another bucket into the cauldron, steam rising from it, and was bending over and splashing the hot water over his face and now bare chest, washing himself.

The washing had been before eating, and Buck lay there in the cold as the sun sank away and the fires swelled and they dipped stew from the other cauldron and took their places near the fire's warmth on chairs they had lifted from the trailer hooked up to the rusted truck. The boy with the ball had returned by then and was sitting beside the small man, who wore a light blanket draped over his shoulders. Their heads were close together and they were talking, and the others were talking and laughing, and the pony, tethered now to a stake driven into the ground, was snorting on occasion, then dipping its head down to the bucket of food they had provided for it. Buck had struggled to his feet and was standing there in full view of them, even in that end of twilight, should they chance to look his way. Saliva dripped from his lower jaw, and he stepped stiffly over the crest where he had lain.

The pony was the first to be aware of him. It jerked its head up from the bucket, snapping the tether taut. The others heard the sound and looked around. Then the pony snorted and they all found him, and though there was a dull gleam in their weary eyes in the growing darkness, he continued on, his tail between his legs now in submission and his head down, gauging each painful step. The plump little girl had risen, uttering a moan and heading toward him, and in a while he stood beside her near the fire.

The others had rigged up an enclosure, poles in the ground and canvas hung between them to form a rectangular room and block the night wind. The canvas glowed red in the fire light and their figures moved in flames on the surface, a shadow play.

She sat on a stool, her head no higher than his, and the warm water washed along his spine and down into his matted hair from either side as she lifted the dipper from the bucket near his tail and flooded him. "Who are you?" she whispered at one point, her lips near his ear, and his tongue slid from his mouth as he panted shallowly. She flooded him again, then soaped him and flooded him again and again, and she moaned through his flinching when the water dampened his scabs and loosened them and there was dark blood in the dirt at his feet where the warm water pooled then soaked down into the earth.

She groomed him, careful of his wounds, using the pony's brushes and her fingers like a soft comb, and his head hung low in her tending, the warm water in his muzzle and eyes. Then came the hand and the metal dish of stew sliding under his muzzle, the steamy scent wetting his nostrils. He ate slowly and without apparent anxiety, no longer guarding his food, watchful of thieves and their attack. Something medicinal then, a tincture, and after that the rough rubbing as she toweled his fur. Then she was working at his paws, pulling away burrs in clumps of dead hair, cleaning between his toes and clipping and filing his nails with small instruments. After a while, when she was done and he had finished eating, she took his head in her hands and turned it and looked into his eyes, then gave him his new name. Later he slept beside her on a soft pallet in one of the tents among the others.

→ELEVEN←

Not at all like languid men who wore their collars up, legs lifted to the running boards of racy roadsters in those twenties photographs of "my crowd" I'd kept but no longer treasured, Avery Brattle sat there like a rock rising from a turbulent sea. But I had been to Gibraltar and had climbed through its caves and seen the tender wildlife, and there was no such complexity in Avery.

"Is that *really* necessary, Christine?"

He meant the meerschaum and the haze in the air between us, so I lowered the pipe to the standing ash tray, smoke still rising from the patriarch's brain, and presented him with a flushed girlish smile, a bit of embarrassment in it, and waited for him to speak again. Then Bret walked in with the tea and cookies on a tray, her hair a nest of snake-like braids above her smooth ebony brow, and proceeded to pour. I crossed my legs, almost lifted a stiff finger to my chin, and Avery, avoiding the heat of this domestic scene, gazed through the leaded windows of my father's study to where Count Southpaw was wrapping his pruned bushes with burlap in the cold. It had snowed lightly the night before, obliterating all animal and human markings. The garden was blanketed in virginal white and the pine limbs were flocked in the manner of Christmas, that holiday occasion not far off.

We'd dated in high school, Avery and I, something urged on by his father and mine. The two were in contemplation of business then. Our relationship had been insignificant for my father, but for his it meant livelihood, and both father and son had pressed it over the years, the latter taking up the cause alone once my father was dead and his had soon followed.

A river separated the Brattle property from my own, a circuitous border. Many tributaries ran into my land from it. The elder Brattle and his Uncle Fritz had been in mineral mining, but had seen the market slipping even before the twenties and had cut their early losses. Fritz had gone back to Florida and the land speculation in which he had earned some money as a youth, while Avery's father stayed on and turned his hand to resort development near the river's edge.

He'd built exclusive lodges and had hired fishing and hunting guides. His clientele had been the wealthy, those wishing to travel into the wilderness from cities to reaffirm their manliness. He'd even put in a small airstrip and had started construction on a fake wilderness restaurant, deer heads and rough-hewn tables, but food of the kind served in men's clubs. Then he'd died, and Avery had counted the money and had shifted it into a weak holding company, letting the mining operations slide into their soon to come failure on their own. Then he'd started waiting for his Great

Uncle Fritz to die. The old man was eighty-seven now, back from Florida and retired, living in a mansion in the busy center of Minneapolis.

The best fishing and hunting was on Pollard land, and my father had allowed access to Brattle customers. The two men were friends, and after my father died I'd gone along with things for a while. But Avery had pressed the advantage, counting on my feminine pliability and ignorance I suppose, thinking back to high school, where he had been a football hero and I, for a time, had been his girl. Men had started to come down the tributaries in large numbers, had built awkward fires on their banks and had shot trees as well as deer. At times they left ungutted, headless bodies in the brush, carelessly happy with their trophy racks.

Avery and I had spoken of these defilements and he'd been quick in his reassurances. But nothing much had changed. And then one day I'd found men at my private fishing spot, a good mile in from our common border. I'd ordered them out, but they'd laughed at me. I was bow hunting and must have looked to them like some Diana or female cupid, at least until I sent my steel point arrow into their inflatable rubber boat. They left then, shivering in their soaked camping gear. From that day on I closed my land to all intrusion.

Danker had kept watch as he was able, but there was too much to watch and he had other duties. There'd been trespassers. So once the homeless were on the move, we'd hired some of them, allowing their encampments near the river's edge, in shacks there or in their tents, paying them with this housing and with food and money. Their presence was unsightly, especially to the wealthy. Avery was right about that, and I'd thought to give in on his promise that the trespassing would stop. But as the Depression had settled on the land, the task of the watchers had become urgent. It was the only work available for them now, an honest living, and I had vowed to continue it, along with whatever other work I could find for them. And in addition to all this, I didn't trust Avery Brattle at all. He couldn't see beyond me as a woman, someone there, first and foremost, for purposes of manipulation.

"Now, Chris," he said. "I'm sure we can work this out without further difficulty. I'm proposing a toll."

"How's Uncle Fritz?" I asked. "Healthy and doing well, I trust?"

"Yes, yes. Fine, just fine," he answered brusquely, his heavy hand waving away the question, blocky shoulders shifting impatiently above his squat frame. His face too seemed a block, expression difficult, as if struggling for release from stone.

He'd brought the papers with him and had rested the folder on the table between us, beside the tea pot and cookie dish.

"Sugar?" I asked. "A ginger snap?"

"No, no," he said, "nothing. But this toll? I…."

"Yes. Like a troll, an exaction for passage. And how would you propose it be administered?"

"Well, you know," he said. "It would be on trust of course. I'd have my man keep a ledger, a count of those going in, the time of their stay. What was taken even."

"And what was left?"

"You mean the cleaning up after?" He touched the folder with his manicured nail. "That's in here too. I've taken care of everything. There's nothing for you to worry your pretty head about."

He couldn't help himself. My pretty head, and my pretty knee pushing through the fabric of my dark stocking where I'd crossed my legs. And my pretty breasts and wrists, and my pipe, pretty too, since its pretty stem was in the ashtray and not between my lips. I lifted it and fished the metal instrument from my jacket pocket and began to work at the bowl, reaming and tamping, then looked up from under my bangs before I reached for the matches.

"My pretty head tells me it's time for a smoke, Avery. Time too for you to be toddling off. You can consider the border permanently closed. I'm saying this officially. You've got hundreds of acres back from the river, and that'll have to be enough for you."

Unable to understand the intractability in a woman's resolve, Avery Brattle called often in the ensuing weeks, a time in which deer season came and went and winter set in heavily on the land. Blue Lake froze solid, and after I'd taken his first few calls I refused the phone altogether and gave my attention to preparations for ice-fishing. No wanderers held residence in the shack now, and after we had worked it through the shore grasses, Danker and I put our shoulders into the task and muscled it out to the lake's center. I'd cleaned and stocked it with food, blankets and drink, and once it was in place I started in with the large auger, which took a while since the ice was two feet thick. I spent my mornings warmed by the shack's coal stove then, fishing in the ghostly blue holes. In the evenings, after we'd eaten the catch of bluegill and perch and the other things Danker's imagination had led him to prepare, we sat over brandy in my father's cozy study, discussing the day's matters, the coming holidays and our preparations for the servants' quarters.

The rooms had been out of use for many years, ever since my mother's death and the end of those social gatherings that gave her life whatever meaning it might have had.

"There's only cleaning," Danker said. "A little furniture and bed repair."

But there were few wanderers now in the serious winter. Those unencumbered by family, and families too, had pulled up stakes and headed south. Only the two men we'd employed as river watchers at the Brattle border remained in residence on the land. Some others passed by from time to time, looking for food and work, but there was nothing left to be done in the gardens and Danker could offer them only odd jobs. They did the work, most usually with care and efficiency, then headed on their way. When the servants' rooms were ready, they sat empty, awaiting the spring thaw.

I spent most of my afternoons at the cabin, reading and going through papers and correspondence. Hans Bonnefoy wrote from New Orleans, where he had returned after spilling the beans about the brutality and suicides at the prison. He'd instituted his claims again, advised by a lawyer that the document in which he'd signed them away was now invalid. "I have little hope," he said. "But I have a job now, at a men's clothing store. You'd like our wares." I wrote back, offering my assistance should it come to that, but I'd not heard from him again.

Some consultation correspondence came my way, a few letters offering work at prisons in parts of the country where I'd never been and some from unknown places abroad as well. I turned them all down. I was sick of the work, not sure if the illness might be permanent. And I felt a need to reconsider my allegiances, given this Depression and my recent experiences. I was feeling comfortable being back home again and took to thinking of these days as moratorium. I looked for mention of the kid in consultation offers and in newspaper articles about escapes, but there was nothing.

The end of nineteen-thirty-five was quickly approaching and with it my Christmas Eve birthday and preparations for the party. There had been one as long as I could remember, not a birthday party, but a gathering of those neighbors and local business associates my father had wished to keep in close enough entanglement. The wives of these men were my mother's designated friends, and their children, including Avery Brattle, were thought of as being on my guest list, even those I'd disliked in grammar school, coming to a better understanding of their detestable smarminess only in the higher grades, once I'd become a maverick.

Now the party was mine, an inheritance, as much as the land and money were, and I'd continued it beyond my father's death, but as a more riotous affair. There was no need anymore for the businessmen and politicians, but the neighbors still came, though I'd cast out a broader net of invitation that included Danker's friends and those previously thought of as unimportant. I still asked the smarmy crew, a perversity I guess, but now my own real friends were invited as well, those home for holidays spent with their parents and all too glad to get away from them for a while.

I'd moved the date to the twenty-second, allowing for a day of recuperation before Christmas Eve and those family responsibilities. The carpets were rolled, my father's prized ornamental stone table became a bar, hats and scarves hung from the bronze statue of Helios prominent in the huge foyer. Danker saw to the liquor and wine and the flying in of oysters and lobster from the East Coast. I made mounds of steak tartare; bowls of caviar sat on tables beside Champagne in free-standing silver buckets throughout the house.

There was dancing, drunken sleigh rides and snowball fights, and the discrete smoking of opium and marijuana in the upper rooms. We stationed hired servants costumed in high school colors and lettermen sweaters at the door of each bathroom, and a large fire blazed in the hearth. A band played the oldies. There was nostalgic necking in the byways of the maze beyond the gardens. It was a ripsnorter of a party, and I could feel the buzz of anticipation in the air across my acreage a good month in advance of it.

I was sitting at the desk half surrounded by windows in the bay at the end of my father's study filling out invitations. The study was at the house side. It commanded a full view of the front gardens and the maze beyond, this morning places both fairyland beautiful and strangely tortured.

It had rained in the early morning hours, some warming out of the south, and I'd awakened to the pinging in dawn's first light and had watched the rain freezing into glassy tubes encasing branches and twig tips. It was a sight to see, clear at first, then brought to a shimmering opacity as the rain froze on the window pane beyond which I was standing in my woolen night gown, feeling my nipples come erect from stimulation of the fabric. Then there was no more to see, and turning to the bed in concentration on the pleasures in my breasts now, I touched and lifted them in my hands, then felt something, foreign and special as the freezing rain, but not beautiful. There was a node there, deep under the surface below a nipple's budding, hard, but not painful.

The pines glimmered in a dressing of diamond ice. Weighted down by it, their limbs had spread to a semblance of glass flowers opening in the sun. Icicles hung at their tips, clear pearls dripping, and beyond them the junipers in the maze had fallen under the ice weight to lean against each other, forming a crazy geometry. I saw a steamy geyser rise above them. It was Count Southpaw, his hose snaked over the ground at the maze entrance. He was spraying hot water to save them before they broke in the strain, and even as I watched I saw the shower of crystals fall, a juniper returning slowly to the vertical.

I was dressed to pamper my new fragility, the black silk Tokyo kimono and soft leather slippers from Batavia. I tapped a finger on a fresh invitation. Then I heard the chimes as the clock struck nine. I'd been waiting for that, and I lifted the phone and dialed Muffy Butterfield's number in Hayward.

"Jesus, Christine," she said. "Hold tight. I'm leaving right now."

→TWELVE←

I'd known Muffy since we'd found an affinity as party prank-sters in high school. She remained my best friend and was the only one besides Danker who knew of my prison masquerade. She too dressed for her business at Bo Peep's Candies in Hayward. She'd been educated in nursing in Chicago in the same years in which I'd been to school there, and we'd examined that lively city together often. The nursing had ended because of her distaste in working for others and the bad language, learned from her father, that had caused trouble even in high school. Her father was not a wealthy man, but he'd stood behind her and had fronted some funding when she'd gotten the idea for the candy shop. She'd made a good deal of money over the years, theatrically catering to the tourists, summer and winter, and through mail order. She stood in a window on main street in her costume, her staff stirring a vat of fudge, and when she was not doing that she was busy ringing up her fortune at the cash register. With the coming of Depression, business had fallen off, but she had a cushion and had become a fixture in that window, now as a promise of future leisure and indulgence. She kept that torch burning in the face of strife and difficulty, though she complained about it incessantly.

"Son of a bitch!"

I heard Muffy's voice, unmistakable near the maze mouth. When I looked up from the invitation I was writing, I saw Count Southpaw bending over to help her, his tall figure slipping a little on the ice where she had fallen. She still held her staff, its sheep hook in the air, and I could see some encrustation on the pole. She was waving the Count away, fighting to rise up on her own. Her bonnet had fallen to cover her entire face. The two of them got her to her feet, and Southpaw held her puffed sleeve discretely as she yanked at her skirt, the hoop swinging like a slow bell above a clapper. She set her bonnet then and stepped lightly along the icy pathway toward the porch. I rose and went to meet her at the door.

"Holy shit!" she said. "Christine, I'm a fucking mess. Have you got any coffee?"

We sat in my father's study sipping from our cups, Muffy a disheveled flower on the leather couch. Bret had been busy with laundry, and Danker had brewed the fresh pot. He'd taken a peep under Bo Peep's hoop as he set the tray down. Muffy caught him. She still wore her bonnet, and it framed her licentious smile.

"Don't you just wish," she said, and Danker winked at her and grinned, then turned and left the room.

She wore patent leather shoes with large silver buckles that accentuated her thin ankles. She was shorter than I, but thin and fit. We hunted and fished together often, and her stealthy grace was evident to me even in that ridiculous outfit. Her staff leaned against the couch at her side, and I could see the encrustation of fudge that started halfway down. She saw me glance there, then smiled and lifted the staff and extended it across to where I sat in the desk chair facing her.

"Peel a bit," she said. "What the hell. I didn't even stop to take the scum sleeve off."

The fudge had softened in the room's warmth, and after my taste I licked the sweet, brown smudges from my finger tips.

"Good," I said. Then we both rose and went up to my bedroom for the examination.

She'd brought two books along, a *Gray's Anatomy* and a large text on gynecological practice. We sat beside each other on my bed and studied them. Muffy had taken her bonnet and skirt off, and the ruffles of her sleeves rose and fell as she turned the pages, pointed to diagrams and read paragraphs aloud. We spent two hours at this, reading and marking passages with slips of paper for future reference, then we went into the adjoining bathroom, where I removed my kimono and stood naked and facing her in front of the full-length mirror behind the door.

My breasts were small, but full, and in no way precious to me, yet in the hands of men they might have been thought of as smart and perky. The aureoles were dark, and the nipples still thrust up, even though the globes had surrendered a bit to gravity. And the separation between them was graceful, even provocative in the right dresses, the ones I saved for parties and occasional nights on the prowl with Muffy. For me these were harmless outings. I'd had my share of a number of licentious boys in high school, then Danker had gotten wind of my promiscuity and had taken me aside and talked to me like a perfect mother. My own mother had her hands full with my father and his demands and was aware of little else. There had been two older men in my early days in college, but since then, for almost ten years, I'd been chaste and not minding it. My study, then the demands and masquerade of my profession, allowed time and circumstance for little else, especially the foolishness of romantic intrigue. In addition to that, most probably because of it, I had no taste for the subservience of marriage or its attendant and necessary pregnancies. I was happy in my life, though in accordance with my culture I could only be half-happy, and I had no care for those possibilities I'd rejected.

Muffy stood before my slightly swaying breasts, and before I could completely settle myself and see into the mirror in my slight embarrassment, she reached out and lifted them, each resting in a palm of her upturned hands, the nipples close to the pads at her wrists and almost brushing them. I felt the absence of their light weight and stood more erect. The globes wobbled a bit, then pushed forward toward her chin until I could feel the tips of her fingers under them at the creases where they met thin flesh at my ribs. It was, of course, as if she were holding ripe melons, musk or cantaloupe, or gourds, or even small cabbages, prize tomatoes, knockers, boobs, jugs, a pair of tits, or the other childish names men had for them, or maybe just these fine, and in my case thwarted, animal factories of motherhood beyond such metaphor. She lifted and weighed them, and I looked down at her studious face, my nipples poking up in the air between us. They were reddening into a hardness and swelling, and when I felt the heat and dampness on my forehead and between my thighs, I looked away, only to see our faces, her cupped hands and my breasts resting in them as a still image in the mirror just a few feet away.

"Steady," she said, her voice a whisper, that breath a cool stimulation, accelerating the ripening. Then she lowered my left breast to let it hang, and making a five-legged spider of her right hand she reached out for the bud crowning the one still balanced on her palm and encircled it.

I could see the red paint on the nails at her finger tips, her white cuticles. The spider wore spats, and its feet pressed down now into the aureole, the nipple swelling out to touch them. But it was no spider, only Muffy, and she was kneading and searching, stopping in brief consideration, then moving on, squeezing the underside of my breast, her fingers digging in, looking for deep evidence.

"Am I hurting you?" she asked. "Here?" she said.

"No," I said. "There's nothing."

"Fuck," she said at one point. "What an asshole. I forgot to wash my hands!"

I'd felt the slight stickiness, a spill of coffee moistening the film of sugar she'd used in her fudge making, but she'd been deep in her concentration and hadn't noticed it.

"I think I found something," she said. "In the other one, but it was deep and I couldn't quite tell."

I was leaning over the sink, sudsing my hanging breasts and pressing the nipples for their relief. When I was clean and had turned and was toweling myself, she spoke again.

"I could tell fibroids," she said. "At least a good guess. But I don't think it's that. But, shit, Chris, I was *only* a nurse, and that was a long time ago. What the fuck do *I* know?"

"More than I."

Muffy stayed on for lunch. Danker was solicitous, knowing something was up. He helped Bret serve in the main dining room, a lovely soufflé, cold cucumber salad, and roasted potatoes. He'd chilled a fine chablis and he poured it into the best crystal.

"He'd make a hell of a wife," Muffy said, her smile tentative across the table.

She hugged me at the door, tight and long, and said she'd be calling in the evening. She'd check in Chicago, even with her ex-husband, "that pecker-head." Her marriage to a handsome intern had been brief, ending in part because of her behavior at social gatherings. She was not cut out to be a doctor's wife.

"Don't worry," she said, knowing the words were useless. I watched her move down the steps and the pathway Count Southpaw had chopped the ice from. She wore her bonnet and hoop skirt once again, her staff held like a javelin above her shoulder. She turned and waved when she reached the door of her red Duesenberg roadster.

I waited until Muffy called and we'd eaten dinner, then I asked Danker to come sit in my father's study and told him the story of my ambiguous condition. The story had not really begun yet, and that was at this point the worst part of it.

→THIRTEEN←

I heard enough of winter storms, frozen plumbing and the repair news that was brought to me in tenderness by Danker, Muffy, and the girls where I lay snug in my hospital bed. For a time I was infected and delirious, fleeting images of home below my forehead.

Tallahassee brought *National Geographic* magazines, Virgo a lap-held reading stand she'd covered in a needlepoint pattern. We discussed articles and fashion and the new issues that had arisen in the radical La Follette administration, the way the country seemed to be shifting even further to the left. Bret baked light and nourishing cakes and cookies, carrying them into my room always with a smile, and even Count Southpaw rode into Chicago with Danker on a few occasions, bearing jars of canned fruit and the first fresh vegetables of the season.

They brought everything I needed or could imagine wanting, but what they brought only exacerbated my nostalgic longing, for fishing and hunting, walks in the woods, that annual sighting of the first hearty buds and returning birds. The Christmas party had been canceled and with it my breasts and the whole of the serious winter. It was mid-March when I returned, and it was either Danker or Muffy who had removed the dresses with low necklines from my upstairs closet. Then it was day trips to Minneapolis, mercifully closer than Chicago, for the regimen of experimental drug therapy treatments Muffy and my father's influential name had arranged for. The smell of camphor lingered in my clothing and with it came thoughts of my breasts and their location, most probably floating in jars of formaldehyde, to be lifted out and dissected by medical students in their study of cancerous tumors. Then my hair was falling, and I had a focus of real concern, something to deal with on a daily basis. I was coming around the doctors said, but it was hard to trust the men who had butchered me.

Only those closest to me were aware of the nature of my surgery, and though I'd acquired a few wigs, I took to wearing silk scarves wrapped into turbans in the old style of the late twenties to cover my bald head. I'd been fitted with a prosthetic device, an awkwardly pointed thing, and I opted for the more conventional mystery of loose silk and cotton shirts. When Avery Brattle showed up, uninvited, I received him in my father's study. He was there in real concern. He had enough sense not to mention the river. He noticed my turban, but only smiled at the quirky choice. The rest sent letters, but were put off from proposed visits. Some mentioned the Christmas party and *that* loss.

In Minneapolis I spent a lot of time sitting in rooms waiting for the chemicals to take hold, the rush of nausea and the headaches, and in those times, after I'd sent Danker away to his searches for interesting Scandinavian foods, I thought of the multiple ironies in my situation. In consultations I had wrapped my breasts to hide them, which had been, in a way, unnecessary, for what man would imagine a woman's breast under the shirt of another of his kind. Now I eschewed the prostheses, counting on the mystery of breasts to carry me through. The men would imagine them there, free and hanging plump below the veil, provocative precisely because they could not see them. Most made images of women anyway, dimming the lights to mystify their reality. My life of work, that essential part of my life, had been masquerade, a woman below a man, and now I found I was doing a similar thing in hiding the denuded reality of a woman damaged toward visual masculinity beneath clothing. The turbans were similar to the bush outfit and the hats, idiosyncratic diversions, like sleight of hand in which I was sending the attention elsewhere to avoid detection of the trick. I was somewhere under there, in both confusions, and there seemed little difference between them.

Spring came on in fits and starts and with it moments of uncontrollable weeping in the primitive fear that I might not see another. There were late snows and killing frosts, but by April's beginning the buds had taken hold and those from the bulbs Count Southpaw had so carefully buried were pushing through in the garden plots, some looking suspiciously like my gone nipples. I didn't miss the idea of my breasts as evidence of my womanhood, only their physical presence, that phantom brushing at my arms when I was washing up, the absent need for their consideration in the act of dressing. Once the bandaging was gone, I looked hard at my scarred chest in the mirror. Each cut seemed evident there, conflated from the third dimension into a scheme on a flat plane, like an architect's drawing in reverse, no guide to building, but a detailed record of demolition. Long and hard. Then I closed my blouse as if it were a curtain over the stage of a ruined theater set and tried to get on with things.

I was sitting below the front porch, at a table Bret had prepared for me, hot chocolate in the thermos and my cup and a plate of oatmeal cookies within reach. It was the first of May. Thin clouds filtered the sunlight high above. I'd been up to the cabin a few times, getting my legs under me again, but this was the first time I'd tended to my pale body. The temperature had reached only the mid-fifties, but there was no chilling wind, and I was wearing shorts and a halter top, a skull cap in place of my turban. I moved a thick towel to cover places on my body as they heated up, letting the sun wash over others. I'd brought a book down with me, but hadn't opened it. I was watching birds in the pines and looking out for squirrels and chipmunks. The junipers in the maze were still at their tips, and I could see the flitting figures of sparrows darting among them and could hear their cacophonous clatter. Then I saw them scatter as the ball rose up among them, paused for a moment, then fell out of sight again.

It was the size of a soccer ball. Even at my distance I'd seen its geometry and colors, red and black triangles as it rotated. Then it was there again, off to the side a bit, closer to me, and a moment after it disappeared below the trees' tips, I heard a faint pinging. It rose up in another place then, further away. It was searching to find its path among the tree-lined corridors, and as it climbed into clear visibility, always pausing at the apex as if looking around, it seemed motivated in the construction of a drama, the tail end of some suspenseful story searching for its conclusion. I saw it rise a last time, higher and much closer now, and I followed it up to where it paused, turning its blinking colors as if they were lighted by some electrical source. It fell from that impossible suspension then, to bounce on the head of the boy who stood, ragtag and mocking seriousness demeanor, a large dog beside him, at the mouth of the maze entrance.

The boy was nodding. With each bounce his chin came up, then dipped, and this became immediately contagious. I found I was nodding too, as if we were acknowledging agreement about something seen or said. The dog was nodding, looking up toward the boy's face and above, watching the ascending sphere. It had a large head and might have been mean looking, but for its lolling tongue and perked ears. They both stepped forward then and moved up through the garden paths, feet and paws in the gravel Southpaw had carefully raked.

The boy wore a pair of ragged bib overalls, nothing apparent underneath. His bare arms and shoulders were hairless, and his cuffs were turned up in thick folds so that his thin ankles looked like sticks above the red and white tennis shoes. He was smiling at me and not at the ball's flight, still nodding, and when he stepped from the garden's last path and onto the clay of the parking area, his neck seemed to telescope down between his shoulders when the ball landed, to be caught on the top of his head for a brief moment before it bounced up, only a few feet this time, then fell to ping on the ground near the dog's muzzle.

The dog stepped quickly forward and jerked its head, sending the ball up again, but not far enough, and the boy caught it in his palm, then turned slightly and bent over and presented it for the animal's appraisal. Then he flicked his wrist and cast it into the air, watching its ascent. When it fell it landed on his forehead. He bounced it twice more, the second time quite high, then put his palm out at his chest and nodded to me. The ball landed on his hand, then was beneath his arm, and his empty palm made a low sweeping motion and the dog stepped forward and crossed its paws in the dirt and bowed deeply from the shoulders, rump high in the air, its tail a stiff pole belying such subservience. The boy stood looking down at the dog kindly when he spoke his first words.

"Still in training, Miss. He's called Young Lyle. Young from Cora with a question after, the ladder in answer of the Master Comrade."

His voice cracked in the second sentence. He couldn't have been more than twelve years old. I saw his arm come up and the ball drop from under it. He caught it on his toe and let it sit there.

"You're very good at that," I said.

"Each according to his abilities," he replied, flipping the ball to his other foot.

"But what about this Master Comrade? The two seem at odds."

"They do, Missus. But it isn't so. The 'fore mentioned abilities? He is a master entermanure. He's our comrade even so."

"I understand," I said. "But what brings you here? Where do you come from? Would you like some cocoa?"

"From Dearborn, Michigan," he said. "Member of the polyterritans. I'm here as emmersary, or advance man if you like. Is there much sugar in it? I like sugar."

"Indeed, there is," I said. "And here are some oatmeal cookies too. Would your dog like something?"

"No'm. I mean, I don't know what he'd like. He don't ever tell me, only Cora."

"Well, sit down anyway. He can sit where he wants to."

"Thank you, Madam," he said.

A clanging came from his pockets and behind him as he moved across the clay, the ball rolling before him now, and took the chair across from me and perched at the edge. He saw my curiosity. Young Lyle sat on the ground a few feet off, the ball between his paws.

"Just trade tools, Miss," he said. "But there's no cup!"

"You're right," I said. "What would you think of using this one?"

"I don't care," he answered. "But taking it from you, it isn't right."

"I'm completely finished now," I said. "Here, let me pour."

I saw his eyes brighten a bit as he watched the chocolate flow from the Thermos lip. His hair was very short, just a blond fuzz. There were blemishes and insect bites along his thin arms.

"Being mother," he said, wistfully. "That's dear old mom, what she would say."

"Where is she now?" I asked.

"Long dead," he said. "Father too. 'Twas the River Rouge union clash. Master of Industry and the Burgazee. 'Ford Gave Bullets for Bread,' according to the lingo. A red banner and a picture of Mr. Lenin. March seven of nineteen and thirty-two."

"Jesus Christ!" I said. "The bourgeoisie?"

"The Lord's name," he answered. "The MC argues against such things."

"Taken in vain?"

"No, Madam, not that. The existence of same is all."

"Ah," I said.

He sipped his cocoa and nibbled at a cookie. I felt I was in some novel from the past century. I'd seen this quality of clothing and demeanor in travelers and the homeless on the streets in cities, as if there were some common reduction in them, a retrogressive retreat to universality in the beleaguered. But I'd spoken to none of them, and this boy and his dog had set the terms of our repartee. I'd entered it, as if into the current quality of his life, easily. Maybe that long experience in prison consultation accounted for it, or it may have been my recent disfiguring surgery. I was conventionally vulnerable, outside there in my shorts and skull cap. Yet I felt no embarrassment or guarding, nor did I feel I was in a foreign circumstance, even though the opulence of my house stood up, accusatory behind me. The boy was looking there, evaluating, but not measuring the real distance between us, and when I looked down at the dog he was smiling up at me, quite contentedly.

"It's not a bad life after all," the boy said. "So long as there is pleasure of entertainment in it. And this gets me to the reason for my being here, Madam, and the offering."

"I've been wondering about that," I said. "Is it for housing and food?"

"No, Missie, though we don't ever turn that down without considering. We prefer money. For services rendered. Said services are of the circus type, a wonderful show, tailor-made to your needs."

"And where is this circus?" I asked.

"Over yonder." He nodded his head back behind him, in the direction of the wood and my cabin and the disputed river.

"And just where is your encampment?

"I can't name the place," he said. "It don't have one that I know. It's in a glade near a river."

I wondered if Avery Brattle had sight or wind of them, rel-, ishing the idea that he might.

"Set up properly for performing?"

"Oh, no, Miss! We come to you, tailor-made!"

We struck an agreement then, for a brief audition show on the following day. I'd been thinking about my coming out party for a while, and this could be just the thing to get me beyond my hesitancy. Only a few people knew of the radical nature of my surgery. No one else would ever know as far as I was concerned. Others were told simply that I'd been ill and was recovering. I'd canceled the Christmas party and felt cheated of it. I'd noted that same feeling under the conventional get well language in the many cards and letters I'd received. I wasn't sure of the timing or the troop's schedule, but I didn't ask the boy about that.

"I'm feeling bad," he said. "We've come along, but I've not yet done an impressive thing."

"*I've* been impressed."

"Well. But it's your hat. It's fit for the ball. Would you stand up for me, Missus? Something to report to the Master Comrade?"

"Okay," I said. "I wouldn't want to disappoint the MC. Will Young Lyle be in it?"

"Yes," he said, rising with a clanking to his feet. "He'll be the polyterritan audience."

He took my hand and escorted me to a spot near the center of the drive. He was quite a bit shorter than I, and his hand was at a level with his chest as he held mine, walking at a distance from me in order to avoid the fabric of my baggy shorts. When he had me where he wanted me he turned. As he walked away I saw the implements attached to loops sewn into his bib overalls below the crossed shoulder straps, a sickle and a ball peen hammer, two heavy carriage bolts and a horseshoe. There were things in his deep pockets too, and they added weight and dimension to his thighs, causing a slight swagger. He raised his arm in a gesture, and Young Lyle kicked the ball from his paws. It rolled toward the boy, then out of my sight line. When he turned I saw it was tucked under his arm again. He was twenty yards away from me now, but his voice was quiet and intimate and I could hear his words without trouble. The sparrows were singing in the junipers in the maze, and a light cool breeze tickled up my thigh under the shorts, then fell away.

"Finding the range," he said. "You might have to move, Madam, the first time. Just a bit forward, or maybe back."

"Right," I said. "I'm ready."

"Ready," he said and lifted his arm. The ball fell and hit the ground beside his foot. He kicked it, and it rose up to his right shoulder, where it bounced, then drifted over his head and landed on the left. He moved slightly to the side and looked up. When the ball fell down again it struck his forehead and I heard that now familiar pinging. Then he was nodding as before, the ball bouncing off his pate, rising up a few feet only. He was not watching it. He was looking at me, smiling, and I was once again infected by that nod and knew that I was nodding too, smiling back at him.

"Here it comes," he said.

I heard the ball slap hard against his head, then saw it rising to describe a graceful arc as it came towards me. I was confident about the range. I stepped forward and braced myself. The ping was a loud shimmer in my ears, and before I realized the smarting, I saw the colors turning at a distance from me as I sent the ball back to him.

We did that for a while. At times I caught the sphere upon my forehead and saw momentary stars, but for the most part it landed on my thin skull cap, bouncing from my bald head. He acted out no tricks, but for the obvious one we were involved in, and after a while, comfortable in our exchange, I found I could loosen my focus, on sound and even vision, could move the intensity of concentration elsewhere. I saw the facets in the cocoa cup and the thermos. The colors in the broad striped towel hanging from my chair arm were intensely vivid. I glanced at Young Lyle, whose eyes were following the ball's trajectory, his tongue lolling to the side of his mouth, pink and moist. I could hear other bird calls, distinctly, through the sparrows' loud clatter, could smell the faint burgeoning in the new buds.

Then I saw the boy reach down into his deep pocket, his other hand behind him at the waist, and in a moment a brass door knob was in the air before him, together with the sickle, sun flashing from its blade, and what looked like a worn leather change purse, all circling in a maze of motion at his chest. The knob seemed heavy and easily controllable and the purse's rotation was rhythmic and regular, but the sickle flashed erratically in its own idiosyncratic sphere, turning much quicker than the other two as he juggled them. At times he tossed one or another high in the air, then took it back into the ordered matrix of activity. He could be cut by the blade, I thought, knowing at once that would not happen. It's just a bit of theatricality, a hint of danger. Then the doorknob was coming at me, rising up with the ball, in a arc just below it.

"Catch," he said, matter of factly, and I felt the cool weight land in my palm just a moment before the ball reached me and I sent it back to him again. Next came the purse, weighted down with nuts and washers shifting in the leather between my fingers, and just after I'd caught it he spoke once again.

"You might want to drop one of them, Missie, either one. It don't matter."

It was the purse, and once I'd glanced down to where it landed beside my foot, then looked up again, I saw the sickle turning slowly in its approach and knew in that moment a complete trust. I lifted my hand, saw the tip and the sharp half moon under it coming at me. The blade rotated in the air, until the business end was pointing in the boy's direction. Then I felt the slap of the wooden handle against my palm. I raised my hands, the knob and the sickle, and shook them. He had caught the ball and tossed it. It was spinning now, in a haze of color at the end of his index finger and he was grinning. He bowed then, and I lowered my hands to my sides and did the same, deeply and from the waist. We'd set our appointment for the following afternoon at three. He disappeared into the maze, Young Lyle at his side, and I saw the ball rise above the junipers one last time. I realized, only when he was gone, that I'd not gotten his name.

→FOURTEEN←

"I don't even know how many," I said. "Or what they might be bringing."

"Six, I think. And a dog and pony."

"I saw the dog. His name's Lyle, Young Lyle actually. You had to be there."

Danker sat at the other end of the table, the venison stew between us. The doctors were urging red meat, and he'd been forcing it on me in collusion with Bret. She and her brother had left for home, but not before she'd cooked what Danker had ordered. It was a hearty, country stew, onions and potatoes, carrots in thick gravy. I had no taste for it and wasn't eating. He was eyeing me sternly.

"Hey," I said. "I'm doing fine. I've got muscle." I touched my fingers to the flesh below my clavicles.

"Even so, Christine, you've got to eat. Have more stew. It's pretty damn good."

The experimental drug regimen had come to an ending. They'd found no more cancer, but I still had to travel to Minneapolis once a week for tests and physical therapy. My appetite was coming back, though my hair wasn't. I felt my pate each morning, searched for fuzz, but there was nothing. Danker was smiling across at me in the candlelight. I wasn't wearing anything on my head.

"There's a nice shine," he said. "High on the phrenologist's chart."

That got me laughing. I lifted my wine glass before sipping and Danker lifted his.

"They're camped near the river," he said. "A couple of patched tents, a trailer and an old rusted pickup. Some ride in the back, I guess. I don't know about the pony. They're orderly enough, as if they've been doing this for a while, traveling I mean."

"Can they be seen from the Brattle side?"

"I don't think so."

"That's too bad."

He was forking through his stew.

"We could stable the pony."

"No problem," I said. "And the dog wouldn't be a bother."

We were both thinking about the empty servants' quarters, ready and waiting, but didn't speak of that. He'd gathered my enthusiasm for the boy and knew of my boredom. I'd not been to the cabin in a long while and was missing my fishing. The mail had piled up, and though Danker had shuffled through it looking for important things, there had been nothing but the get well letters, no real stimulation for body or mind. Another letter had come from Bonnefoy, but I'd not opened it yet. In the weeks after surgery,

I'd rallied quickly. Then the drugs had begun, and I'd weakened. The doctors said it was only natural, but Danker had had to force me into my clothing. I'd been lying around, convincing myself it was recovery and not depression.

After we'd finished eating, I went to my father's study and called Muffy, inviting her out for the next afternoon.

"Sure, Chris," she said. "It sounds like fun."

"You'll have to close the shop early."

"What the hell," she said. "I've had enough of these snot-nosed little bastards anyway, what few straggle in these days."

"Now Muff," I said. "Remember, you're Bo Peep."

"Right," she said. "Bo Fucking Peep."

I hung up the phone and was startled when it rang almost immediately after.

It was Bonnefoy's voice on the line and that startled me once again.

"Didn't you get my letter?" he asked.

"Yes. Right. It came. But I've been ill."

"Oh," he said. "I'm sorry. I didn't know that."

There was a brief silence on the line.

"But I'm feeling much better," I said. "Where are you?"

"It was in the letter. It's strange, strange to hear you. I'm in Hayward, not far away I think. I wrote it in the letter. My grandfather died. He died and left a good deal of money. I'm here to deal with his estate."

"Jesus. I didn't know you had one. This is something."

"It surely is for me. It could solve everything."

"What was his name? Your grandfather, I mean."

I was hesitating, putting off the decision I'd already made. There'd be yet another now to know of my professional masquerade, and I realized that was not professional at all. Still, I trusted Bonnefoy's discretion, but for reasons of intuition only.

"Brattle," he said. "Fritz."

"Good Lord!" I said. "Are you serious? This is more than you know. Can you come out here for a visit?"

"That's why I phoned," he said. "And I have news about the kid. But is it okay? Really? Are you okay?"

We made arrangements. If I didn't call, he should expect Muffy at the hotel at one-thirty. I described her car.

"Is he cute?" she asked, when I phoned her back.

"He's got almost twenty years on you. And he may well be a homosexual."

"Yes," she said. "But is he *cute*?"

I have no belief in the significance of dreams, but that night an image of the kid came to me and I regretted, for the first time in what seemed a proper connection to my body, the loss of my breasts and wept for them.

We were in that fetid room in Naco, the nameless boy was juggling at the foot of the bed, and Young Lyle had been recognized as the lost Buck, the kid's own dog, but not by the kid himself. It was dark in the room, but I could see the sickle flash in the air and could hear the dog whining for tenderness beyond the coverlet. Both boys were looking at me, one down from above and one at my side, and I was offering the milk to them, though my hands were empty vessels. And that was all of what might have been the dream, and I recognized then that I was awake and sweating in the scar creases in my flattened chest, longing vaguely for either of them to take hold of the breasts that were no longer there and suck from them, though both were too old for that. The weeping began then, in coughs that cleared phlegm and sinuses in what seemed a healthy flooding, and when I turned in my sobbing the kid's image slid back into the chair my body had made for him, tangible as the pillow I held pressed into my stomach as I drifted away toward sleep.

I awoke invigorated in the early morning before first light and set about preparations for coffee. While it brewed I gathered up the neglected mail and magazines, then drained a first cup, left a note for Danker, and set out for the cabin in the dawn, chipmunks scurrying across the rough path ahead.

I was a little weak and shaky when I got there, but after a hot shower and a brisk toweling on the open porch among the blue jays I felt strong and centered, if a little tired, and went inside and brewed another pot, then confronted the stack of mail I'd dropped on the desk.

I read Bonnefoy's letter, nothing much there but what he'd told me, though the Brattle name was in it. It was shocking to see it in his hand all the way from New Orleans. Then I fingered through the magazines, prison journals and a few slick fashion rags with beautiful women in their costumes and breasts on the covers. Muffy was there, her coy motherly smile under the Bo Peep bonnet in her new mail order ad. All the women in disguise, I thought, and what a good faker she is.

Danker had opened the bills and paid them. The receipts were in envelopes, date and check numbers noted, and besides these there were only a few get well cards, nothing professional and no consultation offers. Good enough, I thought, and pushed the mail aside and went to the gun rack and pulled down the old twenty-two.

I fired off a few rounds in the woods beyond the deer dressing apparatus. It was the place where Danker had taught me to shoot when I was a kid and the tin cans were still there in a rusted pile. I missed more than I hit. The gun felt odd against my shoulder with no breasts involved. I'd have to work on that.

"Get anything?" Danker asked, when I got back.

He was sitting on the porch drinking his coffee and waiting.

"Just a stitch in my side and sore legs."

"It's a start."

"You're right," I said. "It felt good to be back."

I took a brief nap in the late morning, then dressed in twill slacks and loafers, a checked flannel shirt, and the Mexican belt of silver disks and links I'd purchased in Bisbee in a time that now seemed long ago. Once again I eschewed the prosthetic brassier, but decided to give one of the wigs a try. It was a good one, human hair and well fitted and a color close to my own lost tresses. I felt ridiculous when I saw myself in the mirror.

"You look ridiculous," Muffy said, though she too was over-dressed for the occasion. She wore a severe little business suit, a subtle taupe set off in conscious irony by a pair of red come-get-me heels.

"I know," I said.

"Well, take the fucker off then, Christine, just do it!"

We were sitting on the porch in a half-circle facing each other. Bonnefoy was grinning at Muffy's language. I could imagine what she might have said on the way out. When I'd stepped from the porch and extended my hand to greet him, he'd pulled me into him for a hug and had whispered in my ear, "I thought so." He'd not made reference to my gender since then. He was dressed in a tan cotton suit, fine and baggy in what I took to be a New Orleans fashion style. His shoes were alligator, and I wondered if he'd purchased them after learning of his inheritance.

"From the shop," he'd said, noticing my appraisal. "I quit before I left."

I pulled the wig straight up above my head, then tossed it into Muffy's lap. She jumped in her chair in mock pleasure.

"A Muffy muff!" she squealed, then sunk her hands among the fibers.

It was quarter to three and we were waiting. I'd called the

Southpaw number earlier, to invite the girls, but Tallahassee said they were off to the library and couldn't come. Both took part in "study projects" constantly.

"What is it now?" I'd asked.

"For Virgo it's furniture, Edwardian. I'm looking into primary source material, *las ruinas de Chichén Itzá.*"

"Wow," I said.

"Well, there isn't much. But new papers are waiting. They sent them up from the University of Chicago, but just for a few days."

"I get it," I said. "I'm sorry you can't come."

"But you'll tell us about it later, Chris? Vividly?"

"I'll do my best," I said.

The sun had warmed the cool day, and the clay parking area below the porch was bright in it. The only shadows, those cast by the high junipers in the maze, covered Muffy's roadster. I'd had her park it off to the side to give ample room for the performance. Danker had brought us iced coffee and a slab of the smoked northern pike he'd gotten in Hayward earlier. There were squares of tan toast on a plate beside it and an earthenware bowl of green olives. He'd started off again once he'd put the tray down, but had seen my look and paused for a moment, then leaned over and whispered in my ear.

"I'll be back in time for their coming. And she's right, you know, you do look better without that thing."

I'd pressed his arm, then turned back to Muffy and Bonnefoy.

The kid had escaped once again from the Pearce prison. They'd held him just seven months this time. Bonnefoy knew little of the particulars, but then neither did the prison authorities. They'd fortified the cage area, kept it constantly lit and guarded. He'd entered the outhouse-sized shack in the late evening, but hadn't come out in the morning, and when they looked there he was gone. They'd found no trace of him in Naco or the other border towns.

"But I hear he made an impact at our place."

"How do you mean?" I said.

"More escapes. And that, together with the investigations underway? They won't be in business very long."

"And you?" I said. "What about your legal actions?"

"That's on hold. All energies are in this Brattle business now."

"Isn't *that* a pisser," Muffy said. "Hans told me all about it on the way out. I'll bet the rod up Avery's ass is quivering mightily right now."

"Why?" Bonnefoy asked.

"Because he thought *he'd* get the old bastard's money, that's why. I hear he was counting on it."

"Where did you hear that?" I said.

"Jesus, Christine. You know I get the word at the candy shop. From the old crowd? Even those snooty high school assholes drag their kids in. Everybody talks to Bo Peep!"

"Hey!" Bonnefoy said. "Listen."

I thought at first he meant Danker and the squeak in the screen door as he came through and took a seat beside us. Then I picked out a whistle and its slide into a low register among the various bird twitters. The sound was woody and wet, the tune no tune at all, but a kind of meandering searching for a song. It was coming from somewhere in the maze. I looked to the entrance way, two junipers standing as sentinels at its mouth, then saw Young Lyle step from the shadows and into sunlight. He was swatting the boy's ball with his paws, rolling it on the ground before him, and he was followed by the boy himself, who was juggling, four objects in the air now at his chest, the ball peen hammer, the purse, and two small crystal balls that sparkled. Then came the pony, urged from behind, its head dipping as it pranced to the center of the parking area and stopped and snorted, then curled its blond tail to the side and shat a steaming pile of road apples upon the ground. This caused the figure in dark clothing at its rear to jump to the side, a tall thin man who flung his empty hand toward his shoulder, his fingers gyrating. There was a poofing sound, from his throat or clothing, and a bouquet of colorful flowers appeared in his fist, the petals slightly wilted, stems sagging down to touch his wrist. He stepped further to the side. The boy too had paused, still juggling. Young Lyle stood below him, one paw on the ball now. Then came a plump little girl. She was dressed in a tattered tartan outfit, plaid, pleated skirt, white jumper with suspenders and knee socks, patent leather shoes and a black beret perched on her head. She was whacking at a small ball attached to a wooden paddle by a long rubber line. She kept missing it, the ball bounding off her thighs and arms, and once she'd come to the pony's shoulder she gave up on the task, then crossed her legs and curtsied and reached up to the animal's halter.

There was a brief pause in the action then, the magician and the girl and the pony in a tableau and the boy stationary in his juggling. Young Lyle was like some commemorative symbolic statue at his side. We could smell the pony's shit, ripe and pleasantly earthy, and could hear the flute among the bird songs as it found the tune, Cole Porter's "I Can't Get Started."

"I could dance to that," Muffy whispered. Bonnefoy chuckled, and Danker said, "I'll bet you could."

Then came the man and woman in their full-body tights and muscular arms and thighs and behind them the Master Comrade in disheveled tails and stovepipe hat, playing his flute.

The man carried the woman, her body displayed like a ship's masthead or a hood ornament above his head. Both were blond,

Nordic looking and very fit. Their faces were deeply lined, and I guessed they were of an age, as one might say, possibly even into their seventies. The man held her with confidence, but I could see his arms quivering slightly. There was a film of sweat from exertion on his brow, and after he'd carried her around in a small circle, displaying her, and had moved to the pony's shoulder, the girl still poised on the other side, he lowered her to the ground with some obvious relief, letting her fall the last few inches. She bounced on her toes, sent us a broad smile, then raise her arm in a curved gesture to match his. Their feet were crossed at the ankles in a stance reminiscent of some ballet position.

Now they appeared as a poised team, the pony flanked by the girl and the acrobats forming the central quartet. The magician stood off to the left, near the pony's rump, and the boy was even further back, close to the formal garden's edge, still juggling, the dog alert at his feet.

Then it was the Master Comrade's turn. He took it with the flute only. He was small and quick in his baggy clothing and his hat seemed ready to tip at every turn, yet he moved with grace among them, dipping his body from the knees like a jazz musician. "On the Sunny Side of the Street" now, as if he'd left all worry on the doorstep, then moved up to stand beside the little girl and played for us, winding out of the song with a good deal of flourish and filigree. He lowered the flute to his side when he was finished. Then he bowed, and each of the others took the cue and bowed too, even the boy and Young Lyle, the former juggling on what seemed an impossible horizontal plane as he bent over. The girl had pulled at the pony's halter, and it too had been forced to bow.

"All right, all right!" Bonnefoy yelled out, uncharacteristically. "Let's hear it!"

We on the porch applauded loudly, our several enthusiastic claps distinct from one another because we were so few. Then we waited for what was coming next and found it was the Master Comrade and his spiel.

He was shorter still when he removed his stovepipe to reveal a bushy head of salt and pepper hair that matched his thick eyebrows. A little portly and slightly bow legged, he stepped downstage a bit and stood in front of the pony. Then he looked at his hat, now in his hand, as if he'd just discovered it there and didn't want it. He shrugged and tossed it over his shoulder. It sailed beyond the little girl and was caught in the extended fingers of the magician, whose flowers had disappeared. He held it by the brim, brought to waist level. A wooden stick was in his other hand, having materialized there when he'd extended that arm to show a white cuff. He'd extended a foot too, and when he raised his toe I saw the shoe's sole, pulled free of its stitching and resting on the ground. The MC turned and looked along the porch to both sides, as if there were multitudes there. Then his eyes found us, sitting at the center, and he began his speech.

"Ladies and gentlemen," he said. "We live in troubled times," *ka-BOOM*. It was the magician. He'd rapped the wooden stick against the stovepipe brim, which had the quality of a snare drum now, its dark inverted chamber providing volume, and the slap of his foot against the shoe sole was the bass, deep and impossibly resonant.

"Did you get that, Lyle?" The MC called out over his right shoulder.

"Each according to his abilities!" It was the boy, his familiar voice at a slight distance. He was still engaged in the juggling. I saw the ball peen hammer kick up high in the air above him as he spoke. The dog sat on the ground beside him, the ball a few inches from its paws.

"Lyle!" The MC smiled, punctuating the name as introduction, *ka-BOOM* again, and his eyebrows twitched. "And the stately

animal sitting at his feet? Let's welcome Young Lyle!" *BOOM*.
"He's younger at least than Lyle is."

We clapped again, watching as the Master Comrade disengaged himself even further from the others, stepping forward to
speak more familiarly.

"All here are the products of these troubled times. You can
see Lyle's craft, this masterly tossing learned on the streets and
stoops of Dearborn, Michigan. But his real skills are utilitarian,
lest entertainment become that in troubled times. He's exception-
ally adept at river and lake fishing, a fine caster. He's done some
trapping too. You might say, a city boy? But it's all true."

He turned then, his head wobbling on his neck as he
searched for, then found the little girl, then extended his hand in
presentation of her.

"Cora!" *ka-BOOM*. "This child comes to us from God-
knows-where. She doesn't remember."

"Name of the Lord taken for exclamation only!" It was the
boy again, his voice a punctuating chorus, this time a small crystal
ball rising.

"That's right. And came to us quite beleaguered and without skill. She raps the ball on the paddle, of course, at times striking it."

He'd moved to her side and was now squatting and struggling to lift her, his arms gathered at her hips around her tartan
skirt. She held her paddle out in the air over him and the ball was
bouncing off his head and shoulders. Then he had her above the
ground and was staggering toward the pony, and in a moment her
body was plastered against its side, her free hand reached for the
mane. He was pushing at her behind and chunky legs. The left one
was kicking up to gain purchase on the pony's spine. The animal
had spread its own rear legs to hold steady for her awkward mount-
ing. Then, after considerable pushing and grunting from both of

them, she crawled up onto the pony's back, shifted her hips and rose to a sitting position. The Master Comrade moved away, then turned to face us again, raising his arm to the side in presentation of the pair. The magician sounded another *ka-BOOM*, though this time a tentative one.

"There you have it," the MC said. "No cowgirl, but we can promise a pantomime skill. We call her The Animal Care-Girl. That's the real talent, and needful, for animals remind us of our own helplessness and that we better damn well be thankful that we are human and have our resources. This pony, she'd called Blondie, and Young Lyle, the dog, both came as extreme images of our own plight, Blondie as superannuated from a ragtag riding operation that couldn't afford such indulgence for the pleasures of children anymore and Young Lyle from among those desperate travelers less fortunate even than we."

The speech was long. He was winded from the exertion of lifting the chunky child, and though the magician was poised and ready, it was Young Lyle and Blondie who filled the moment of silence. The dog barked and swatted the ball as if it were some toy he'd animated in imagination, and the pony pawed at the earth and snorted, then threw its head. Cora reached to its neck and petted it, then the MC called out again.

"George Brankowski!"

There was no *ka-BOOM*. The magician seemed startled, as if the order had been altered and he was not ready. He looked down at the hat, then flicked his wrist. The wooden stick was gone. Then he reached into the hat, feeling around in the darkness, and when his hand came out he held a flapping chicken by the feet. I saw Young Lyle's head jerk up, his pricked ears and steady stare. Then the magician crammed the chicken back into the hat, the stick was in his hand again and he rapped out the response.

"We call him GB," the MC said, "and that could be Good

Boy were he young enough. He was a vacuum cleaner salesmen. Might just as well have been bibles or encyclopedias for all the good of it. His magic is trade-trick, helpful in accomplishing entrances to the dwellings of potential housewife customers, quite useless now, for where is the money for such indulgence? He can clean like a whirlwind, even without his accoutrements. We call him Good Boy at such times. That's the utility skill, for cleanliness is close to godliness."

"Only a folk saying. The literal ain't in it!" The juggling boy again, this time the purse rising.

"You've got it!" the Master Comrade said.

The sun was sliding behind the house now and a stripe of shadow lay on the clay beyond the porch. The MC was in the sun, squinting a little, his bushy hair a basket of filtered light. He looked up to where we sat, then stepped forward into the shadow and spoke more softly as if in confidence to each of us.

"You know," he said, "we're earthbound. And even the earth these days seems headed on destruction's course. There's winds blowing the top soil, the boll weevil and other scavengers. Some say it's our sins, bound to be that. I don't believe it. The innocent children fall, like Cora and Lyle here. The aged are innocent too, for the most part, and those of us on the middle ground, a working class with no work, are just trucking on to make ends meet. We'd fall into the earth, unless we kept moving. It will be our sin, to speak figuratively, if we don't take up the children, lost animals, and the aged along with us.

"Still, there may be hope in entertainment, and a lesson too. For there are those who fly! They can still do it, get free of this beleaguered earth, an example for all of us, and maybe a taste of coming revolution. Ladies and gentlemen...." He stepped back out of the shadow and turned again. I could see the poised stick in George Brankowski's hand.

"Amy!" *BOOM.* "And Bob Darling!" *ka-BOOM.*

The old couple disengaged themselves from their long held pose, a little awkwardly from a stiffening of muscle and sinew I thought, as the MC drifted into the background on a slide of mincing steps, giving them center stage.

The woman's hair was grey and gathered into a bun, and Bob wore therapeutic cuffs. Still it was not he who squatted down and made a cup of hands, but Amy Darling, her back straight in the tight tank top, spine distinct where it descended between the slightly sagging halves of her buttocks. She called out a signal of some kind, a huffing sound, and Bob clapped his hands together at his chest. He was facing her squatting figure. He stepped forward on one bent leg, extended the other out straight behind him, then dipped into a low stretching position. Then he stood up straight again, bounced slightly on his toes, and reached out and touched her shoulders, tapping them, then stepped back a few feet and slapped his thighs. Then he extended his arms in graceful gesture and shook his fingers and wrists.

They were going through some pre-trick exercise that was at once that and a business of drama, urging our expectations. It was done by rote, but the communication between them seemed fresh and real, something enacted many times before, in their youth perhaps, and now they were renewing that youth, or at least their long standing commitment to one another.

Bob Darling hesitated, was poised, then broke away from his ready posture and stepped to the side. Amy called out again, her head nodding sharply down toward her cupped hands. Her indistinguishable words now sounded like "Come on! Come on!"

Again Bob took his position and again he shook his arms and wrists. Then he stepped forward, reached down and touched his fingers tips into her shoulders and lifted up his foot, tentatively. He pressed it into the stirrup shape she'd made for him, settling his black slipper there with slight ankle adjustments. I saw Amy's own slippers shift on the ground under her haunches, securing the purchase for a final time. She grunted again, sharply and with a guttural groaning, then lifted her head and looked into Bob's face as he leaned down over her. He moaned in response, both resignation and trust in the passive sound.

They were finally ready, as were we, and before we could linger in the moment, Bob was flying up into the air, stiff as George Brankowski's stick. His arms were tight at his sides, but when he reached the apex of his climb and was falling backwards in the beginning of what seemed a reverse somersault, his right arm shot up straight above his head and we heard the slap and saw, a moment after, the crystal ball in his hand. Then he was spinning and we heard the other slap and searched for its source in Amy, a momentary misdirection. When we looked back to Bob, he'd touched ground with a slight bounce before settling. The ball was resting on his palm, at the end of his extended arm. His other hand held Amy's, and her crystal ball had risen in a similar gesture, out in the air on her palm beside her. They both grinned. She curtsied and he bowed, and before we could applaud we heard Lyle's voice again, back in the distance, "It ain't magic, but skill!" The Master Comrade stepped forward then, once again to center stage.

"Well, there you have it," he said, "our audition in these troubled times. It ain't magic, just as Lyle said, but skills that take on added importance in their needfulness. *We* need them, just to get along, and maybe you do too, if for other reasons. The Darlings that you've just witnessed? They too, like Blondie, are from a failed circus, though they left it well before it slipped down into the earth as so many other endeavors these days. They became farmer-gardeners, in retirement after years of hard strife on the trail of the American Dream. That's much like the Christian Message, you know: do the work now, get paid off later."

"So much for the Christian Message!" Lyle called out.

"That's right! He knows. At any rate, as the man says, what you see is what you get, and you can have it all for very little indeed. This group of comrades. A little desperate. Just a little hungry and tired. We are at your disposal. You can have us for almost nothing, or whatever you see fit."

→FIFTEEN←

The troop moved into the servants' quarters a week later, after days of erratic weather, a killing frost, then freezing rain beating on the windows followed by snow flurries. The sun came out again on Thursday and with it warm air from the south. By the weekend, buds were showing again. Monday was the fourth of May, and with the troop's coming spring seemed to have dug its heels in and taken hold.

I was in Hayward, lunching with Muffy and Bonnefoy, when they took up residence, and it was left to Danker to spell out the terms of our agreement. He'd spoken to the Master Comrade about the early solstice party I had planned, something to replace that canceled Christmas do. I'd set the date at the fifteenth of June.

We'd be expecting their entertainment, not necessarily a formal presentation. We could work that out later. In the meantime, we could make good use of what the MC had called their utilitarian skills. Count Southpaw could always use help with the gardening, and Bret and the girls would welcome assistance with the spring cleaning that was coming up.

In words passed with George Brankowski while he was preparing a stall in the stable for Blondie, Danker learned that they'd been on the move without respite for the past two years, since Cora was six and Lyle only ten. They'd gotten this far north without a plan, just following business where it led. They'd been sacked once or twice, losing goods to roving bands of thieves, nothing essential to life and livelihood, and they'd come away without injury. GB thought they all needed a rest and some temporary permanence of place. At least he knew he did.

"What about the Master Comrade? What's *his* name and story? And what's Cora's? How did they find her?"

It was seven in the evening on the day of their arrival and I'd not seen one of them yet. They'd turned down dinner and so had I, over Danker's stern protests. We'd eaten lunch late and too much of it, Muffy, Bonnefoy and I. Danker was sitting across from me over martinis in my father's study, a tray of crackers, aged cheddar, and niçoise olives between us. I could hear the dull hum of a vacuum cleaner in the distance. I'd taken off the head wrap and prosthetic bra I'd tried for the day. I was completely bald now. Though the regimen of drugs had come to an end weeks before, not a hair had grown back. There was a window open somewhere, and the cool breeze felt good on my scalp. Danker was watching me.

"Chris," he said. "You really do have a nice looking head there."

"That's good," I said, "since you may be seeing it for quite a while."

"I'm not kidding. It's classical. Like a statue."

"Well," I said. "I'll have to figure something for the next prison consultation. If there is a next one."

"Do you think there will be?"

"I don't know," I said. "Not yet. But what about this crew?"

"Well, the MC? He prefers that. Brankowski was the first one to join up with him. He thinks he knew his name at one point, but he's forgotten it. By the time the Darlings came along and they started their performances it was Master Comrade, or MC. There may be something in his past. George thinks so, but he doesn't know what. Lyle came after Blondie. They found Cora when she was four years old, but the age is only a guess. She was sleeping in a hay field in Kansas. Maybe someone had abandoned her there. She had little with her, rags and a cache of rotting fruit and cheese. It's mysterious, George says. The dog joined them about a year ago."

Muffy had been uncharacteristically subdued at the start of lunch. She'd had a run-in with her chocolate supplier and was feeling bad about it.

"I didn't give him a chance," she said. "I was bitching and moaning, acting like a stallion's ass. He has his own troubles, four kids, and on the road constantly. He's just trying to hold it together. Shit, what a bull-headed fool I am!"

"Unfortunate images," said Bonnefoy drily.

"That's right," I said. "Let's stick to gender."

Muffy loosened up a little then, and by the time Bonnefoy had started in on his inheritance and the Brattle business, she was grinning attentively, her elbows on the table, eating up the gossip with the roasted muskie.

Bonnefoy was Avery's cousin once removed, his father product of a dalliance more than a half century before, when the

Louisiana prison was the viscount's castle and a place known for its satisfying bacchanals. It had been Avery's grandfather's brother, the recently dead Fritz, down in New Orleans working in the family's Mississippi shipping business, who had found his way there and into sexuality with Bonnefoy's grandmother.

"I always thought it was the viscount himself," Hans said. "Probably he had her too. At any rate, the information, a few letters and documents, were among the old man's papers when he passed on, along with the will that left most everything to me. I'm the only living heir in his direct line. It seems solid stuff, that information."

Avery had tried to squelch the will, but he'd gotten nowhere, and days after Bonnefoy received the startling information a letter from Avery was in the box.

"It was an obsequious and obviously guarded thing. He proposed that we get together when I came to Hayward."

They'd met twice since Bonnefoy had arrived, once for lunch and another time for dinner at Avery's hunting and fishing lodge near the river. The will gave Hans plenty of money, but it gave him land too, a good hundred acres just north of the lodge compound.

"He needs that land, for his outdoor business. I've not decided about that yet."

"You'd certainly have him squeezed," Muffy said, relishing the possibility. "Chris on one side, you on the other."

"That's right. I know," Hans said. "And he has no money to buy it from me. More important though, he doesn't seem to have any heart for it. His business I mean, and maybe it would be good if I bought him out."

"Good for whom?" I said.

"Well, for *him*. He seems in a bind."

He'd gotten the lay of the land and had been shopping, exchanging his loose New Orleans clothing for rough-and-ready wear, the best around. He wore a fine flannel shirt, heavy twill hunting trousers and soft leather boots. A silk scarf hung at his neck. His hair was free of oil now and fluffier. Still he moved and gestured in that lazy manner, more appropriate to warmer climes. Muffy was watching him and he was avoiding her glance. I took the opportunity to lift and adjust my fake breasts, to touch the headwrap at my brow.

"He's okay," Bonnefoy said. "Just needs to loosen up a little."

"You bet your ass he does," Muffy said. "More than a little, though."

"Who knows?" Bonnefoy said. "It remains to be seen. We'll be meeting again for dinner, day after tomorrow."

Muffy passed on dessert, saying she had to run. Hans had said his goodbye, then went to the restaurant bathroom, leaving us alone, and I walked her to the door. The candy shop was just across the street, and we were faced with a full-sized cutout of Bo Peep in the window, Muffy's smiling face staring out at us from below her bonnet. It was pleasantly cool on the shady side, the sun cutting through a swath of shadow parallel to the white line.

"Do you see that bullshit?" Muffy said.

"Of course," I said. "It's you!"

"But it could just as well be you, Christine, in your fake tit costume. This is foolishness. Look at these!"

She lifted her small breasts in her hands. Two women were passing, and they looked away quickly.

"Muffy!" I said.

"Crapola!" she said. "They're just useless. There's no children sucking them and only a few men to fondle them, and that's pretty much a bore. And you're *presenting* them? You look much better anyway with a flat chest."

"I'll take it under advisement," I said.

"And the head wrap too. Get rid of that."

It was four days later that Hans Bonnefoy arrived with his luggage. Muffy drove him out, but had to get back to the candy shop and left immediately. It was a warm, dry morning, no breeze to speak of. We took our coffee on the open porch, nibbling at the pastry he'd brought along from Hayward. There had seemed no good reason for him to continue on at the hotel, especially now that the house and grounds were occupied with the MC's troupe. One more would make no difference. I'd lost solitude, but was enjoying the activity. I was coming back strongly from the surgery and treatments, but was still considering the new image I'd be presenting to the world. A bit of the world at home might help. I could try various ways. Muffy had glanced approvingly at my cashmere sweater and floppy hat. The former hid nothing, and the hat rode high on my hairless brow.

The Darlings were poking around at the edges of an elevated plot in the garden beyond the parking area. Count Southpaw was standing over them, hands on hips, appraising the quality of their considerations. Both were dressed in tight elastic outfits that looked like long underwear. Bob squatted beside a plant, carefully pulling the burlap away. Amy was on her knees studying weeds and pulling some. Bob grunted in a manner reminiscent of their act, and we saw her look up sharply in response. The vacuum cleaner hummed in the distance, then stopped, and Young Lyle came into view from the house side, trotting along. He was heading for the maze entrance with clear intention. He didn't glance up to see us as he made his way past the Darlings and Southpaw and through the stone pathways winding among the new green buds and perennial topiaries. We watched him until he disappeared at the juniper tree entrance, then I turned to Hans for more talk about Avery Brattle and the kid.

"How was the dinner?" I asked. "Any progress?"

"Can't tell yet," he said. "We're going down to Chicago end of the week."

"What for?" I asked.

"Well, the lawyers are there, and we thought we'd take in a show or something. We'll stay overnight, then return the next evening."

"Oh," I said.

The kid had been out of sight for two months, though there were constant rumors as to his whereabouts, gossip generated within the prison culture among both officials and inmates. At Pearce, the escapes had continued at a good pace.

"I hear they've put up some sort of thing they call a Vision Fence and have installed some mirrors beyond the walls. I don't know what they're for."

"I do," I said. "But it's obviously too late for that."

"Too late for anything," Bonnefoy answered. "Once they see the possibility realized, they get heart, and there's very little that can stop them then. Witness my old place. He certainly started something there."

"But the question is, what do they get out into?"

"You mean this Depression. But it has to be better than the other."

We talked a while more, then Bonnefoy rose to go and freshen up. Danker had placed him in a bedroom on the second floor, two doors down from mine. It had a nice bay window that looked out over the woods, a private bath and sitting room attached. It had been Danker's digs, and though I'd not asked him to vacate the space, he'd insisted, moving his gear to the first floor, near the servants' quarters where the troop was ensconced.

"It's better," he'd said. "I can run the place more efficiently from there."

He'd been spending a good deal of time with the group, instructing, but socializing too, and he was my source of information. I'd stayed clear of them. I'd traveled up to the cabin most mornings and afternoons, where I'd worked on my fishing gear, repairing lines and tying new flies, resting and going through the mail and preparing the invitations for the early solstice party. I'd decided on a masquerade ball, Wisconsin style. All ice was gone from the lake and rivers and the oak buds were popping. Soon the trout would be ready and waiting in my favorite pools.

Danker arrived on the porch soon after Bonnefoy had left. He was carrying a pot of fresh coffee. When he saw that Hans was gone he took the vacant chair across the table from me.

"Do you think a trio, or a full orchestra?" I said. "I've thought some twenties music, nostalgic stuff for the high school gang."

"I'd go for the Big Band," Danker said. "We can rent rooms in the hotel in town. I'll set food and drink in your mother's sewing room and the back library. They can rest there between sets. Throughout the night, I'd imagine?"

"Not quite," I said. "We're not that young anymore."

Count Southpaw had left, and the Darlings were both on their knees now, heads close together. Amy was clipping away at dead growth, while Bob cleared mulch near the bush's base. Then he dragged fresh fertilizer from a burlap bag and spread it. We could hear those grunts and guttural calls and clicks.

"Do they ever just talk?" I asked.

"Oh, sure," Danker said. "But they do that business much of the time, especially when it's between them."

We heard a dull whapping from the rear of the house.

"He's beating the guest room carpets," Danker said. "That man is a tornado! He fixed one of the vacuum cleaners for better suction. He's polishing and dusting everything in sight. Out of sight too. Bret and the girls seem stunned."

"He pulled a nickel out of my nose," I said. "That was after he'd gotten the scarf free of my ear."

"Practice," Danker said. "They've been conspiring in the evenings, blocking things out I guess. How much do you want from them?"

"I'd like to keep it loose. Nothing formal, just during lulls in activity. Maybe some roving magic, and Lyle's juggling? If it's warm enough, we've got the parking area."

"And the lights," Danker said. "I've checked them and they're working fine."

"Maybe the dog and pony stuff out there. What about the MC, what does he do?"

"Damned if I know," Danker said. "Aside from political introductions and his flute."

He appeared just then, Lyle and Cora following. Cora held her paddle and was dressed again in her tartan outfit, and Lyle toted a sack that hung along his leg. They crossed the clay parking area, stopping for a moment to watch the Darlings at their work. The two looked up at them and smiled. Then, the MC leading the way in his tails and stovepipe, they wound their way down the garden paths and disappeared between the junipers at the maze entrance.

"The dog went that way," I said. "Just a few minutes ago."

Danker laughed. "Maybe it's a Communist cell meeting. There's revolution in the air."

"It's spring," I said. "There's no denying it."

→SIXTEEN←

The invitations were in the mail by mid-May, and only a few days later Danker began to get phone calls and response cards. They'd be coming from all over the country, the high school crowd. Some sent regrets, but not many. A good number mentioned the canceled Christmas party and how this one promised a welcome new life. Nobody balked at the costumes.

I took a few of the calls myself, still guarded about the previous cancellation and my surgery when that was mentioned. A costume could hide everything. I was toying with the elaborate, possibly some high necked Victorian thing with plenty of ruffles and stays. But I was also considering a complete revelation of my state, feeling I'd been in costume long enough, in my work at least, and that it might be time to somehow wear the inside on the out. I'd stood before my mirror naked recently, had studied the scars and contours of my flattened chest. The doctors had done a pretty fair job; I had to give them that. The scars might have been the war wounds of a young soldier.

And I'd admired my head as well, holding another mirror and turning to check from all angles. A few hairs had appeared, spiked and brittle, and after a day or two of hope that I did not really feel, I plucked them out and rubbed some lotion in for a good shine.

The letter came on the first of June. I was up at the cabin going through the mail and waiting for my fishing buddies. When I saw the return address, a prison in Philadelphia that I'd read about, I put the other papers aside and opened it.

The kid was mentioned in the second paragraph. He'd been taken three weeks before at a campsite in the woods near Scranton, and the letter made no bones at all about the concern. The warden outlined the terms of the holding. There was a careful drawing enclosed. More information could be sent along once they heard from me. The proposed task would be a very specific one: how might they be sure about the kid and the security surrounding him. What they were doing now seemed foolproof, but it could only be temporary given state laws about prisoner treatment. They had him chained to a cell wall under bright lights, a guard watching him. The lights were dimmed at night, and the chains were long enough so that he could lie down and sleep on a metal cot. A pillow, blanket, and a thin mattress; that was all. He was docile and friendly, but the guards were instructed not to speak to him. He'd requested a pad and pencil, a few books, and these had been provided. They could hold him this way for another few weeks, but that was about it.

I wrote back immediately, saying they could send the information, all that they had. I could get there anytime after June twentieth. I'd wait to hear from them. Back into the world, I thought, but in what way? Then I heard the tentative knocking at the cabin door. When I opened it the four were standing there, Lyle, Cora, and George Brankowski, all smiling, even Young Lyle.

Away from the Master Comrade, performance and the work that fulfilled their housing contract, the kids were just kids, George Brankowski a city boy lost in the country. He tripped on the trail, spilling creel and poles in a tangle. When we got him to his feet again, he jerked scarves and flowers from his sleeves, a deck of cards and a length of rope from under his jacket.

"I don't know why I brought these," he said sheepishly.

Lyle carried the lunch Danker had fixed for us, and Cora gave her attention to the dog, who needed no attention as he snuffled among the rotted leaves turned to mulch at the oak trunks, acting just like any dog.

"Is it far?" Cora asked.

"Just a little ways. We're going to the other side."

I lugged a canvas bag of towels, the net and stringer, and a can of worms.

The kids were dressed in my clothing. George had found it in dusty boxes in a closed up room on the third floor, things I'd worn when I was their ages. Lyle was in dungarees and a light sweatshirt and Cora in a flowered dress with a low waist that had been in style for children at the time. There had been a country girl bonnet packed beside it, and I remembered, now with some good humor, my mother insisting upon the outfit. It was a little too tight at Cora's broad hips, but she looked better in it than I had.

"Is it bad up there?" I spoke to George. He was behind me and seemed confused by the question.

"I mean in those rooms. I've not been there in years."

"It had use of the cleaning," he said, then nothing more. He was busy with his footing.

We stayed back in the woods, well above the lake and out of sight of it. The shore was overgrown clear down to the water on the far side, and I searched out my old markers, then found the trail that would take us down to the rock outcroppings, a place I'd not fished since I was a child. I'd left my fly rod at the cabin, but had seen Lyle eyeing a casting set and had brought that along. We'd be still-fishing, for crappies and bluegill, maybe a bass or two if we were lucky. Leisurely fishing, most often boring, but good for lazy talking. Young Lyle found the trail before I did, and when we reached sight of the lake he was standing on a slab above the water's edge, ears pricked and attentive like some dog food advertisement. He turned and barked, a woof from his thick chest. We parted the branches and stepped out on the rock. We could see the ice fishing shack, small on the distant shore. The lake was still and sparkling, but a blue-green in shadow of the overhanging trees.

I spread towels on the rocks, then pointed to places near the edge where there was natural seating. Then I horsed up the hooks with wiggling worms and adjusted the bobbers. Cora was the first to plunk her line in, the bobber bouncing on the rocks below, then slipping into the water near shore. Lyle had prepared a green lure for himself. He cast out gracefully to a good distance, clearly skilled in the matter, then turned and grinned at me. I took care of George myself, throwing his line out, then handing him the pole as he was edging down into his rock seat. The bass struck immediately.

"Holy mackerel!" he yelled, and Young Lyle barked.

"Not quite," I said, "but don't jerk it," then left the negotiations to him. He was squatting awkwardly, half seated and reeling, and I quickly screwed the handle extension onto the net and climbed down between the rocks. The fish was hooked through the lip and he was reeling it in too quickly, but when it popped from the water I got the net under it before it fell free. That was the first one, a nice bass at least a pound in weight, and we gathered around and admired it where it panted in sun on the rock. Then I strung it through the gills, climbed down again and dropped the stringer into the water at shore.

We caught bluegill and crappies and a perch that we threw back. Cora caught an eel and a bass almost as big as the one George had landed. Lyle caught more than any of us, but like any wise fisherman was philosophical about his successes. Once the stringer was half full, we broke out our lunch, meat loaf sandwiches, pop and potato chips. Cora kept her line in as we ate. It was noontime and the sun was high, the rock pleasantly cool under our fingers at the blankets' edges. George was dressed in my father's fine fishing gear, canvas pants and a vest of many zippers and pockets, a plaid shirt under it, and a floppy canvas hat set low on his brow. He'd brought a Brownie along and had taken a few pictures. Now he was lounging on his back, up on his elbows, smiling out from under the brim.

"So this is fishing," he said.

Young Lyle had sidled up to sit at Cora's side, on her dress where it spread over the stone. She was scratching his rump with her free hand, the pole in the other. Her half-eaten sandwich sat in waxed paper near the dog's snout, and when she said "Go ahead, sweetie," he edged forward a few inches and nibbled delicately. Lyle sat crosslegged, his back to us, looking out over the lake.

"There's a position of the moon," I said, "where it lays light on the water in a bright stripe that comes right up here and spreads out. You can sit in it. I remember doing that once, with Danker. I was just a kid then."

"I remember the moon," Lyle said, "in Dearborn, up over the buildings when it was quiet at night. When they took me away and it was night there and I saw the moon in the window I thought,

157

gee whiz that's Dearborn, and that's when I got out of there. I was just a kid then too."

"The moon," Cora said, wistfully.

"Good Lord," George said, "it got so difficult so slowly."

"Name taken as common expression," Lyle whispered.

"First it was candy from dishes, food left on the table. They wanted their houses cleaned, that's all. But I kept hope, too long it seems, that somebody would buy one. Just one, and then onto the next one. Then it became objects, just anything I could fit into my pockets. I'd do a little magic, cards and cups, but they were as desperate as I was. Then it was money, and they caught me. I was in that slovenly room, the rent due, and trying to get some sleep. I didn't have relative-one. I'm sure there was a full moon that night, at the window, then the light from the hallway blotted it out when they came and got me."

"What's the first thing you remember, Cora?"

"My name."

"What do you mean?" Lyle said.

"Somebody asked me and I told it. Then they took me away."

"Where were you?" I said.

"I don't know. Outside somewhere? It was night in a prairie or field. They asked me and I told them."

"What about the moon?" George said.

"I don't know. Maybe at the place they took me to."

"What was that like?" I asked.

"I don't know. I left."

It struck me then that they were all escapees, like the kid, but that they'd found something to keep them out for good with the Master Comrade. Then it came to me that Cora was the kid's sister and Young Lyle was Buck, the kid's dog. I thought it first as a bit of fancy, the right ages and circumstances with both. Then I thought that I knew it for sure. And why not. It was powerful coincidence, but so many were on the move these days, crossing paths. It might not be as odd as it seemed at first. I thought of Bonnefoy and Avery Brattle then. That was coincidence of a different kind, but once realized it seemed reasonable. That was it, I thought, like my flattened chest. Who might imagine it, and yet once my breasts were gone reality had taken over and things seemed as they should be. The sickness was in wishing them back again, and I'd stopped doing that.

"What about the Darlings?" I asked. "And the MC himself."

"We don't talk about that," Cora said.

"We do the Darlings," Lyle said.

"That's right," said George. "It's a simple story, Bob and Amy, stage names like mine."

"George Brankowski? That's a hell of a stage name," I said.

"I like it," George said, "close enough to the real one, but far enough away too."

"Mine's real," said Cora. "At least I think so."

"Mine too," said Lyle.

A breeze came up off the lake to ruffle our clothing, then fell away. A few high clouds were in the sky now, the sunlight softer through their filtering, and the shadows on the rocks around us had lost their hard edges. Cora lifted her pole and we heard the bobber plunk down again below us and out of sight. Young Lyle had finished the sandwich and rolled over on his side so Cora could get at his stomach, which she was scratching absently. He groaned and shifted closer to her, his head now on her knee. Lyle had lifted some pebbles and was juggling them in low tosses with his right hand only, his left on the rock beside him. The fish weren't biting.

"The Darlings were taken in a circumstance that came right out of the movies. At least that's the way they tell it, when they tell anything at all," George said.

"Between grunts and moans," Lyle said.

"And those funny clicks," said Cora.

It seems the Darlings had been working a farm near Leonard, Kansas, not in ownership, but sharecropping a plot of vegetables and flowers that flourished in spite of drought and attendant dust storms. They lived in a shack that had been for hogs. There were none left. The farmer had them both out on his wasted land, though the top soil was gone in the wind and there was only clay and the dry, nubby remnants of better years to be turned under before the furrows were seeded and the sky was looked to for a rain than never came. They had a few hours then to work their own plot. They sold the flowers and vegetables to those who still had money. A percentage went to the farmer, not near enough to keep his house in order. He was desperate and infuriated at their meager success.

"He got it into his head that Bob was after his daughter. She was fifteen and wasting away as he was. The farmer's daughter? Bob was close to seventy and Amy was enough for him, but maybe it was because the daughter was losing her promising womanhood before she got to it, through malnutrition that shrunk her breasts and hips, and the farmer latched onto any wish for her desirability. I don't know. Her mother was dead, and it was just the two of them living together there, as if man and wife."

He came out into the dusty wind with a shotgun. Bob and Amy were chopping away at the hard, dead soil. The horse, unfettered from the tiller and resting, all its rib bones visible through the skin of its rising and receding chest, gave a faint whinny, and Bob turned to the warning and saw the girl stumbling behind the man, then heard her raspy and dry throated cry.

"Amy says Bob made it over the horse's rump and into the bare back riding mount old movie cowboy style, but the horse could hardly hold his weight and slumped. Bob dug his heels in and the horse tried to step away and was doing that, but far too late. The farmer fired, hitting the horse, and it fell dead in its tracks, landing on Bob's leg and pinning him to the ground."

The sheriff came with his deputies. They got the horse's body off Bob and helped him to his feet, then shackled him. When Amy saw this she grunted and leaped into the air and caught the sheriff behind the ear with a solid kick. They shackled her too, then took them both, for horse thievery followed by the murder of the horse that had been stolen.

"The farmer told them of Amy's rage at Bob's attempted escape from discovered adultery, that she had shot the horse to stop it before shooting him. They were locked up with other poor souls, all hungry in an overcrowded compound, the women segregated from the men."

"And now they're here," I said. "How did they get out?"

"They just showed up one day, while the MC and I were pitching our camp. He'd been playing the flute and I'd been doing a little magic. They added some dimension."

"Never have they said clearly." It was Lyle. The five stones he'd been juggling each plinked down onto the rock in punctuation until his hand was empty.

"Never have they said clearly, Miss," Cora echoed, and Young Lyle grunted under her scratching.

The sun was sinking beyond its zenith. The clouds were gone now, and the shadows had shifted and regained their geometric edges. Branches from the overhanging trees blew lightly, shifting leafy patterns in their blocky figures. We had a full stringer, and though Cora still played her line near the lake edge below, she was desultory in her plunking. Her face and arms were red from the sun.

"Maybe it's time," I said. "Time to go."

"Fishing," George Brankowski said, once again lounging on his elbows in my father's clothing.

"I remember sitting on the roof in Dearborn. When it was evening? Just remember sitting there, the tar and the chimney pots and sun squares in windows in the distance. Nothing to do." Lyle looked out across the water, his palms on his knees. "That was something."

"I don't remember a thing," Cora said.

We trudged back to the cabin in the late afternoon. Lyle carried the poles and the towel bag and pointed out some good places on the way where he could set traps. George had enough to handle with the net and creel. Young Lyle carried nothing but his renewed energy and alertness, leaving the trail to search in deadfall and among vine covered arbors. Cora insisted on toting the fish. Some were still kicking, their scales lustrous below panting gills on the long stringer, and when she tripped, dragging a crappie across the ground, she paused and looked down at it.

"I've made it dirty," she said.

"Here," I said. "It's nothing," and took the stringer from her and held it up and brushed the twigs and brambles from the fish's body. "Why don't I tote it for a while."

I waited for her assent, not wanting to rob her of the job, and in a moment she smiled and nodded deeply. When we turned again and started after the others I felt her stubby fingers as she took my hand. I raised the other then and carefully slipped the stringer over my shoulder until the burden was riding on my back. I could feel the wetness and the shudders of the dying fish along my spine as we started on our way again, as well as the heat in Cora's palm, and could smell the bitter sweetness of her hair.

→SEVENTEEN←

Preparations for the summer solstice party moved along apace, even as strife continued in the land, and poverty, outside the cities at least, could not be accurately measured. As the air warmed on the continent more people pulled up stakes and, like animal and bird migrations, urged also by weather change, headed out in desperation, not so much to find a better life, but to escape the difficulties of the ones they were in.

Very few found their way to northern Wisconsin. The migration was south from there, by those who had managed to stay alive and healthy wintering over. Some came to the house along with spring and were put up temporarily in the stable stalls beside Blondie, children stroking her muzzle and soft nose, and were fed by members of the troupe, most usually on the porch beyond the servants' quarters. Bret cooked stews and pots of chili and fixed salads, a combination of early vegetables plucked from the Count's garden and from the store of canned fruit, green beans and peppers that filled the basement racks, product of my mother's quiet desperations over the years.

The party efforts seemed a seasonal thing and as such no indulgence. George Brankowski's work went along with the spring cleaning, and the Darling's activities in the gardens, pruning, fertilizing and clearing away mulch, were just natural preparations for summer growth.

"They're talking to Southpaw about growing corn," Danker said, "though they might not be here long enough to taste it."

"Why do you say that?"

His comment pulled at me unnaturally. I knew I'd be missing them when they were gone, though I'd spent little time among them, but for the increasing occasions of fishing and woodsy explorations with the children. They came to the cabin freely now, interrupting my work and ruminations, and I welcomed that. I'd been teaching Cora the names of summer birds as they returned, and Lyle and Young Lyle were very good company.

"Only the seasons," Danker said. "Things change."

We were in my father's study once again, going through lists and commenting upon them. It was early afternoon, but the Southpaw family had left already, though they'd be coming back again. Danker had been in a cooking mood for days, and he'd planned a dinner to include Muffy and Bonnefoy and the Southpaws too. Hans had promised to return early, at least by five. He'd been spending a good deal of time with Avery Brattle, and he was at his house now.

"Consideration of possible agreements," he had said.

Something was going on, and I had my suspicions. I heard a

quiet whinny. When I looked out through the window I saw Cora exercising Blondie, walking her around on the clay drive. Young Lyle was trotting at the pony's heels.

"She certainly has a way with animals," Danker said.

"Yes," I said, still watching her, those thick legs in my childhood overalls.

We went through the list of food and drink, then considered the major things that were still to be done. The parking area would be a performance and snacking space. Danker had arranged for speakers to carry the music out from the large dining room, where there would also be dancing, tables and chairs pushed to the walls, the carpets rolled. There'd be an elevated bandstand in front of the fireplace at the room's end and outside, at the clay perimeter, tents under which food and drink would be available. We'd staked out a small meadow to the side of the long drive in, just a hundred yards or so from the house itself, for parking.

"The grass should be cut," Danker said. "We'll need lights along the entire way."

"It'll get dark late. Some will leave when it's still light."

"The older, sober ones," he said.

We'd decided to station the same young men at the bathroom doors. Their lettermen's sweaters would be their costumes.

"Have you reached them?" I said.

"Almost all. A couple aren't available."

"Okay," I said. "Isn't that about it?"

"Not quite," he said, "but we've got time."

We heard the front door opening then. It was Bonnefoy.

We drank martinis in my father's study. Hans had changed his clothing and now wore a formless seersucker suit that looked like pajamas. His hair was carefully oiled and combed. I could see his bald spot under the soft lights through the strands. I'd changed into a pleated, cotton skirt, slippers and a loose peasant blouse. I wore a new skull cap, something I'd picked up in Minneapolis on our last trip to see the doctors, who had given me a clean bill of health for the time being. The cap was made of a light woven fabric, colorful and somewhat small. It didn't hide what might be hair, but only accentuated my baldness. "You're going to lose yours too," I said.

"I know, I know. I'm fifty-five years old, or is it four? I'm still vain about it. But seeing you that way? It doesn't seem so bad."

"Maybe you'll get a monk's ring above the ears."

"May be," he said.

Then we heard voices echoing in the foyer and we both rose to go and meet Danker's other guests.

The Count stood beside the statue of Helios, whose torch tip rose above his head. Southpaw had no such accoutrement, but had gathered his women around him and Muffy too. All were clinking their glasses to mark the moment, martinis and the Count's tumbler of fine Kentucky bourbon. They opened like an exotic flower when they heard us coming, Bonnefoy holding my elbow. The Count wore a conservative blue suit and tie, his posture reminiscent of that long ago pitcher's stance, arm loose at his side, leaning in a little for the sign. He was smiling, nodding in greeting. His hair glistened in its marcelled waves. Bret stood beside him in a plaid suit, green ribbons in her hair. She was holding her own, which wasn't easy in the presence of the girls and Muffy too this night. The girls were dressed in dramatically different ways. Their look was only to be taken in slowly, for the savoring, and Muffy wore a simple burgundy dress, almost no makeup at all, her hair naturally casual in a bob. She seemed subdued, but there was brightness in her voice when she greeted us.

"Hans!" she said. "Chris, you look lovely."

"So do you," I said, and turned to the girls, the Count and Bret, and shook each of their hands.

Tallahassee had woven pearls in a braid at her brow and her high cheek bones were touched with an almost imperceptible gold dusting that shimmered. She smiled down at me, her large eyes moistening, one woman to another. Her dress was a flower print, four gigantic calla lilies, their stalks and petals flowing across her full breasts and hips.

"Chris!" she said, and Virgo, always the startling bohemian, in her white silk blouse and the men's slacks she had adapted for her use, echoed my name. Her hair hung in ringlets to her shoulders.

Danker had left us, but now he returned, still wearing his apron.

"Dinner," he said, "is served."

Dinner was rack of lamb, small new potatoes browned in a garlic and fennel mix, and a salad of watercress and dandelion that Danker had bathed in lemon juice, slightly roasted walnut slivers in oil in the mix. We started with a course of tender leeks, sauteed in butter. Four bottles of Lafleur, a Pomerol my father had put down years before, sat uncorked on a sidetable near Danker's elbow, their labels a self-satisfied certainty blinking in the candle-light that lit the crystal goblets, the silver and my mother's best china.

We ate in the large formal dining room, as if in some oasis near the room's center. Danker had separated the table, pushing the other half to the room's far side, where it was dark and the dour hunting landscapes on the walls were only vague squares and rectangles beside the heavily draped windows. The table was very long, and half of it provided ample space for the eight of us. Danker stood at the end, I in a chair beside him, Bret across from me. The Count resided at the other end, Muffy at his left elbow, Virgo at the other. I looked across at Bonnefoy, who sat between Muffy and Bret. He was looking at Tallahassee beside me, her wondrous face I thought, half-smiling as if reconsidering his preferences, and even when Danker sat down, the signal for beginning, I had to tap my fork on the plate's edge to get his attention.

"Oh," he said softly, then joined the rest of us in savoring the leeks.

We were tentative at first, for though Danker had cooked for us before, all but Bonnefoy, it had been in different combinations, never all together in this way, and our larger group would need managing to reach the intimacy I knew we were capable of. I winked at Bret. She had touched Danker on the arm, pointed at the plate with her fork and smiled, a cook's knowledgeable approval of another, then turned her head and smiled at me. She was the soul of the house, for she had been working for us when my father was still alive and had read the spirit of my mother in her knowledge of my father's demeanor and the objects and physical arrangements my mother had left behind. I came upon her, once, in the basement. She was standing among the multiple shelves of preserved foods that were stacked up in careful rows from floor to ceiling. She was slowly shaking her head in wonder, not about the abundance, but the woman who had come to such a state that required it.

"Danker, these leeks are delicious!" Tallahassee said. I looked past her to the table's end, where Count Southpaw was forking up the last few tender bits. What to think about him? I thought, as he leaned back in his chair and touched his napkin delicately to his lips. He has a house full of beautiful women.

Muffy was watching him, her eyes slightly glazed in contemplation. I had no idea what she might be thinking, though I guessed it was something good.

"Muffy?" Danker said. He had risen to gather the empty plates and was now at her shoulder. "Would you please pass the potatoes? And Tallahassee? The lamb platter please?"

We ate slowly, savoring each bite, and soon we were engaged in quiet conversation. We spoke of the coming solstice party, literature and ideas, the Depression. The Lafleur had blossomed in its downtime, and we could taste the subtle varieties in its separations, plum, tannin, and black currant. Bonnefoy sighed, his nose above the glass. Even Danker, usually reserved about such things, smiled as he rotated his stem, admiring the black ruby color of the liquid.

"Maybe this is it," Bonnefoy said. "The solution to all problems."

"It's a growing problem in the cities," Virgo said. "I've read that sales are way up since Prohibition, mostly the quite inexpensive wines and liquors."

"It stands to reason," her sister added. "Like those fanciful movies just now. You can hide away in a bottle or the theater. For a little while at least."

"Or a solstice party," Muffy said, without irony.

"Will they make a movie of that *Porgy and Bess*, do you think?" It was Bret, who had taken up reading in her spare time years ago, influenced by her nieces. Virgo had acquired the libretto, and they had all read through it.

"Oh, I *wish* they would!" she said. "I've not heard the music, but the words are quite fine and intelligent I think."

"It's Gershwin, isn't it?" Danker said.

"That's right," Tallahassee responded. "It's doing well in New York City."

Boulder Dam had finally been completed, and Tallahassee had searched out the drawings and blueprints, which she described in vivid detail. We talked about that and the promise of Roosevelt's WPA project that was in the news.

"What will you all wear to the party?" I asked.

"I'm going to try something dignified, garb of the Mad Hatter or Charles Chaplin I thought," said Danker.

169

"The little tramp, with those big shoes? You better keep yourself mobile."

"Father will wear his baseball uniform," Virgo said brightly. "Won't you?"

"If you insist," Southpaw said, smiling gently at her. "A little shake and rumble. That's if it still fits."

"We don't know yet," Tallahassee said. "At least I don't."

"Nor I," said Virgo.

"I thought something with breasts and hair. That would be a serious costume," I said, and the girls laughed lightly at my boldness. Bret's lips tightened for a moment, like a mother, before she smiled.

"I have no ideas at all," said Bonnefoy.

"*I* have," Muffy said, "but I'm not telling."

"I'll be Queen Victoria," Bret said, "with white makeup," and we all laughed.

"What about Avery?" Muffy asked.

"Well, *he* has ideas, but I'm not allowed to speak about that," Bonnefoy answered.

"You seem to be getting very thick, you two," I said.

"I suppose so."

"I don't hear anything from the river," Danker said. "No hunters or fishermen coming over."

"I was down there the other day, gathering wild herbs," Southpaw reported. "Everything seemed in good order."

"Are there still watchers?" I asked.

"Just the one now," Danker said. "The other headed out. He let me know a week in advance, giving his notice."

"Such civilities," somebody said.

"To hold onto those," Bonnefoy spoke philosophically. "As if a last vestige."

"Of civilization itself," the Count said. "Most who have come for work or food? They've been that way, very formal and dignified. Isn't that right, Bret? Very sensitive about manners? The troupe is that way too. The Darlings are keeping hours, although they divert from them for time with the Master Comrade. But they put in extra time in the gardens then. Nobody's watching of course. We never even talked it over. Somehow, it's a matter of structure, a way to keep a life together."

"And the MC himself?" I asked.

"Good God! Who knows?" Bret said, her hands in the air above her plate.

"Name taken only as exclamation. No implied commitment," Bonnefoy said dryly.

Danker rose and poured the last bottle of Lafleur. He'd baked two loaves of crusty bread, and while we sopped up the juices from our plates, he went to the kitchen, then returned carrying a tray of individual dessert bowls—wild strawberries in cream—two bottles of the 1921 Yquem my father had put down in that year, and fresh wine glasses. He placed the tray on the sidetable near his seat and sat down again.

"Avery's got his mind on other things," Bonnefoy said. "He's not working the fishing junkets with any gusto. Some new ordering of his life? That could be coming."

"Have you made a deal on the land?" Muffy asked.

"Not yet."

We kept talking, drifting from one thing to another without insistence. We were lazy and full of the fine food and wine, enjoying our company in that special way that can release the self, unguarded, though we were not speaking of guarded things. Then one came through, followed by some others.

"Has it wintered over well? At the lake?" Danker asked.

"Well enough," I said. "There's never much change."

"We often went fishing there, when Chris was a child." He spoke to the company by way of explanation.

"What about your father?" Virgo asked. "I don't quite remember his involvement. But that was years ago."

"My mother. All this crystal and silver and linen, a collection in his house. She was an item too, and even then I saw I could become that."

"He didn't care much for women," Bret said softly.

"Or children?"

"I wouldn't say that, Chris," Danker said. "He was a busy man."

"Your friend."

"Well, that's not true exactly. I was always an employee."

"I think I might have been one too, not a very good one."

"I hardly remember my mother," said Tallahassee.

"I remember her," Southpaw said. "She looked a lot like you. Isn't that right, Bret?"

"She did indeed," Bret said. "Something in Virgo too."

"My mother was like a child," Bonnefoy said. "I was her toy, like a doll. But that's a long, long time ago now. One has to grow up."

"How long did it take you?" Muffy asked.

"About fifty years."

They all laughed lightly and so did I, and Hans put on a face of mild rebuke, joking, but serious in his eyes. We could hear the sound of a flute in the far distance, the Master Comrade in accompaniment to our conversation.

"You know my dad," Muffy said. "There's nothing much to tell. He's got a good costume in mind. I'll say that for him. He's a dear man."

It seemed Danker's turn then, and after a brief lull following Muffy's words, one in which we thought of her father's face and demeanor, we all turned to him expectantly.

"All right, all right," he said.

"About your sister? You told me that to correct me, when I was her age."

Danker spoke of her then, her death quite suddenly at sixteen, and how his mother had pined for her and how, for his father, her going had seemed a relief. Danker could be the only child then, a boy for his father's shaping. His mother could take a place in mourning and be put aside. Danker's father had been active in the approach, but I was a girl and mine had assumed the stern, passive role. His look was of dignified disapproval for the most part, and when he did approve I was to see it only in the absence of that disapproval: things as they should be, a proper course. He approved education and seriousness in reading in this way, and hunting and fishing, talk of current events at the table, and clean clothing, and an understanding of the mechanical, all manly things, since they were the only ones to be taken as having weight and thus worthy of approval.

Danker had told me of his sister in order to correct me, that moment of drinking and promiscuity early in high school. The story had been the old one and in my father's Protestant capitalist mode: no carpe diem, but seize the future in the present, be on good behavior, for who knows what might happen.

I hadn't considered that part of it, but that Danker had spoken to me, at least listening to what I had to say, though he had made his judgments beforehand. I'd allowed for an opening, and then he'd taught me the important things, looking for purposes of seeing, how one might read of nature and history and apply the information, the real pleasure of education in the moment.

Was it only that, I thought, to be spoken to and not at? The nostalgia caught in my throat. I could feel my breasts heaving, though they were no longer there.

"Sweet Jesus," Bonnefoy said in a whisper when Danker had finished. "It's all so stupid. And wasteful."

"But it's almost summer," Bret said, turning to look at him. "It all begins again."

The strawberries were perfect, small and succulent, the Yquem luxurious, rich, lightly golden, and big in its opulent fruit and oaky bouquet. We raised our glasses to each other, then scooped up the remaining dessert from our bowls, our spoons clicking on the ceramic. It was close to ten o'clock now, and the distant flute was no longer present in our brief silences. But the rich scent of coffee was, the strong brew steeping in the metal pot Danker had carried in on a tray that held the little white cups and a dish of sugar cookies. I saw Bret's nostrils flair as she breathed in the scent, and soon Bonnefoy's cup was at his lips, Muffy's half-way there.

"Our father was a slave. Isn't that right, Bret? He'd come from Africa directly, though I never learned the country. But Africa, somewhere on the coast I think, and our mother too. She died in childbirth. Bret had too much force and energy even then I guess. Directly from Africa, and that's why I have these beautiful daughters who look like they're from there too.

"My father was a gambler, both before and after he was freed with the others, a systematic gambler with systems and ideas about building them to insure a modicum of success in gambling. He'd lose and then he'd win and lose again. And then he'd win again. He found a balance. Always just a little ahead, he'd have some money in his pocket, enough to give us a few pennies, for candy-sweets and cookies and those other trifles that can go a long way in keeping children happy. This was in Florida where many of the baseball teams trained in the spring, and I used my pennies to gain entrance to their games, loving baseball both because my father gambled upon it and because I found it a beautiful game. I met my wife at one of those games and would have married her immediately after it ended, but I couldn't because I was only ten years old then, in eighteen-eighty-two. By ninety I was married to her though and playing that game and our father was dead. I was gambling too, though not in the way he had, but only on the skills of my fellow players and on myself.

"We'd bet on everything, the number of strike-outs, balls thrown to a particular batter, infield hits, double plays, the final score, even the weather. We'd bet with the other team, for this was the way we earned our money since we received almost nothing from the gate."

"In ninety-five our mother was killed. We were but tots then, Tallahassee a year older than I, and I don't remember it at all. I remember bits of the trip north, bundled up in a wagon, various week-long stops, peoples' faces, and a cold I'd not experienced before when we got here, which frightened me."

"But then spring came and we had a tent by the river. Father learned and taught us fishing and Aunt Bret taught us school work by lantern light. Virgo had friends, farm children who looked at us strangely in the beginning, but got past that and were friendly, but I didn't make friends easily and stayed close to father, helping with the planting of our garden not far from the river's edge."

"I was quite good at that, for some reason. I got seeds and seedlings from the parents of Virgo's friends, which they gave kindly. It cost them almost nothing, but they gave easily, without any beggar treatment, because they liked my daughters, I think."

"He planted everything, my brother did, by the river on what we thought of as our found land, and though the season was short his garden burgeoned with more than we could possible eat. He'd leveled the land against that descent near the river's edge, then tilled it and planted his cycle of vegetables and the cosmos and other flowers to draw the insects away all around the perimeter. He'd found books and seed catalogues here and there. He read them and in a while set up a small farm stand not far from the river, but a good walk. We would all lug the baskets there and wait for the few wagons that passed by. Then a man came and told us the land we were living on was his and that he wanted us out of there. He was not really bad about the news. He gave us a month to pack up and leave."

"That was Robert Saint James, Chris. I see his son and the children, and their children, at my candy store from time to time, but not much since the Depression. They're okay. They've got money still and land."

"I found a man who had been left a widower with four small children, who had a house and some land on the main road leading into Hayward. He was holding fast to the place, fighting foreclosure, doing odd jobs and caring for his children. I proposed a garden near the edge of the road, no investment on his part but seed to begin with, old wood leavings from his barn, and fertilizer from the few cows he'd managed to keep and maintain for their yield of milk. We could split the profits, seventy thirty, with him getting the larger portion."

"That was Gunnar Pfisterer. My brother had dealings with him, before I came to work for your father, Chris."

"That's right. The man agreed, and soon my father had the garden in and we were camping in one of his outbuildings. I played with his children and Tallahassee and my Aunt Bret helped with chores the man's wife had abandoned to him. It was a good arrangement and properly formal, though I don't really remember much of that. My father has refreshed the memory by telling the story to me and my sister in the evening after dinner."

"The garden, I might say, was magnificent, and it got the ball rolling. The farm stand was crowded, wagons all along the fence. Soon people were approaching me, offering work, could I, or might I consider, building gardens for them? Some were the servants of the wealthy, carrying messages from those who didn't, themselves, stop at farm stands.

"The rest of the story is our most recent history, accelerating in a straight enough line until this very moment. I took many jobs and consultations, stayed free of further binding contracts. In only a few years I was able to approach Saint James and offer good money for that place on the river where we had camped and plotted our first garden."

"And that's where we live now, my brother and my two nieces and I, in a house we all had a hand in building. It's a small place, but sound, and it gives out on lovely views of the river. That's why we prefer to sleep there most of the time, though Christine has provided rooms for us here. The river has its sounds, and birds fly and flitter at the shore, and the buzz of insects rides close over its flow in early and late summer. Animals come to drink in winter, their tracks and clean droppings in trails in the snow down to that washing at the edge. The flow itself can seem hypnotic, but it's not really that, because we listen closely and stay awake in bed until we come to release it when it's time for sleep. People come to the house to visit, old friends now. The Lipper sisters come, those old musical girls who taught Virgo and Tallahassee to play so beautifully on the piano near the window and the cello that leans against it. They bring honey from their hives and fruit, and sometimes cookies. We drink honeyed tea together. When it's warm and the days get very long, we often sit on the porch and watch the river change its colors as the sun goes down. It gets a beautiful sheen then, light blue among silvered ripples, and when the sun is almost gone, we can hear the night birds sing."

"Wow." It was Bonnefoy. He spoke softly.

"Wisconsin," the Count said. "It's wonderland."

→EIGHTEEN←

The Lipper twins were the first to arrive and I couldn't tell them apart. They were always early, not from need for attention or any hunger for a fair share, but because punctuality was a virtue and they were virtuous.

I smiled as Norma approached me at the door, but it was Alvina. She was carrying a wicker basket, jars of berries and plums put up by the girls last summer, each tied at the neck with a different colored ribbon and tucked down in confetti. They too liked to be called "the girls," though they were in their late-seventies. They were identical, and though they always dressed in identical outfits down to the last stitch, they were easy to tell apart, but not now.

Alvina wore an ice skating costume, a tight red vest above a flared skirt, and even skating boots, the runners removed, and a black wig cut straight across in Dutch Girl bangs. Norma stood behind her at the porch edge, a lumberjack, complete with checkered jacket and toy axe, her grey hair tucked away in a wool winter hat with ear flaps. She raised the axe in recognition of my costume. Alvina smiled wistfully, appraising the bones.

"Are we early?" one of them asked. I heard the hollow click of beads, as if before a chant, and saw the dour monk approaching in his sandals from my father's study. It was Danker, who had eschewed both the Mad Hatter and Chaplin, opting for subtle and more mobile gear. He was lowering his hood, and he grinned and said "Oh, my!," then accepted the fruit basket gift and placed it carefully on the trestle table beside my cape. Then he took the girls on his arms, escorting them across the foyer and into the large dining room so they could watch the band set up, musical as they were, teachers of the piano, saxophone and stringed instruments.

I stood in the soft shadows at the door. I could see the entire parking area from there, the open space of clay ground at the center and the four colorful tents, under which the hired servants were busy at the tables, fussing with trays of finger food, glasses and bottles. They all wore white, the men in suits, the women in loose cotton dresses, the sleeves of which blew with the tents' fringes in a light spring breeze. It would be warm enough, though the breeze held a touch of coolness as the day began to sink away and shadows edged into the formal garden beyond the clay. Then I heard the soft clop of hooves near the house side. When I looked that way I caught my image in the hall mirror. Sun came from the left and the mirror seemed lighted from behind, and I was a revelation of my private self there.

I was a skeleton, my bones luminescent where they floated like an arrangement of bleached sticks in the voids of my black silk body-stocking. They were not quite articulate, but subject to any motion, all hung or stacked from a still center at the girdle of my hips, which seemed broader in bone than in the invisible flesh of my real self. The silk shimmered as I moved, a hint of artifice. But in the bones' drama the shimmering seemed shadow only, an absorption of the bones' light that thrust them into roundness and protrusion and the illusion of a swelling dimension in the cage of my ribs where they dipped in to meet the sternum much like cleavage, though when I turned into profile it was apparent there was nothing there.

I could see my ear and the orbit at my brow. I'd highlighted the latter as well as the edges of the sinuses above with white makeup to increase their prominence. I'd dusted my cheekbones for the same reason and had oiled my scalp. There'd been a mask provided, but it was too real and a little horrifying, and I'd decided that my head would be an emblem, reminiscent of the kind of thing carved on the surface of a sarcophagus or coin.

Clop, clop. I could hear them coming, the clop of the pony's hooves as if my bones clacking. I wore low black heels, just high enough to push my calves out. I was extremely thin and could feel the rise of my buttocks in the silk holding them below where the visible sacrum dipped between. My cape was a bundle on the trestle table beside the Lipper sisters' fruit. When I lifted it the bright red underside flashed in the sunlight. I spun it dramatically, then draped it over my shoulders.

I stepped through the doorway onto the porch, then saw Young Lyle trotting out at the house edge and Lyle following and juggling, then Blondie's nodding head as she pranced into view. Cora was sitting astride her back, dressed as a plump princess, complete with golden crown and ruffled sleeves, creamy bib and the red, patent leather party shoes I'd worn as a child. Her dress was part of the same outfit. It spilled with thick crinoline, something my mother had urged upon me long ago. Cora grinned in the light makeup I'd helped her with and in the pleasure of my clothing, and only the mitt she held in her lap suggested the kind of ridicule I'd felt in wearing them. She flipped the mitt to the side and Lyle caught it and took it into his juggling, a baseball and a toy bat and the mitt now, and his hat, which he replaced upon his head, then plucked the bill and tossed it up again into the matrix. He was a Tiger from Detroit, in pinstripes and knickers, something Danker had found too in Chicago. Blondie was a show pony, her mane and tail braided with strings of beads. Only Young Lyle was who he was, though freshly washed and brushed out and wearing a red scarf at his neck to match the color of his lolling tongue.

The four paraded in a circle, then turned to face me and came to a stop. Lyle said something, and Young Lyle extended his paws before him on the ground and bowed. Cora touched Blondie's neck and the pony crossed her forelegs and did the same.

I could see Lyle grinning through the objects turning in the air, and behind me, back inside the house, I heard the instruments rise up in harmony in their tuning. Then I heard laughter off to the left, and when I looked down the drive toward the temporary parking area, I saw the cheerleaders coming, four abreast in unison dancing, and behind them a witch in a conical hat, a hunchback and a pilot, Eleanor Roosevelt, and a man with spiked hair, a pistol in his hand and a bloody brow. Then others were coming too. I stepped out to the porch edge to greet them.

The cheerleaders reached me first, four women from the snooty crowd in high school. They did a little choo-choo number for the team, giggling enthusiastically before skipping up on the porch steps. Their uniforms were tight and cut into the fat at their waists. Their little skirts accentuated thighs that had grown thick over the years, but their smarmy smiles hadn't changed much at all.

"Quite stunning," one of them said snidely in appraisal of

my costume as they passed by and entered the house. I heard the music rise up into a real tune, and when I turned I saw them rushing toward the large dining room. I suspected they'd be dancing with each other until "the boys" showed up.

"How the hell are you, Chris?"

It was Brandon Butterfield, Muffy's dad. I leaned over to kiss him, avoiding the bullet hole and the blood that had spilled across his cheek and down his chin and neck. He wore a tattered business suit, complete with tie, stick pin, and vest. There was blood at his collar too. A giant, upright trout was coming up the steps behind him. The fish nodded, slid to the side and entered.

"Product of the crash of twenty-nine!"

It was Lyle calling out in his juggling. I could see him grinning over Brandon's shoulder. The mitt rose above his head, then the toy bat, then his hat. Then the hat was on his head again and Cora caught the mitt and tossed out a small wooden horse. Then the horse was spinning in the air, together with those objects of the Great American Pastime.

"Absolutely right!" Brandon said. "I've committed suicide." He'd elevated his eyebrows with paint, and this together with his spiked hair gave him a surprised look. He was surprised that he'd shot himself, then surprised again at what that felt like. He was waving his revolver, causing curls of smoke to drift out at the barrel. A nice touch, I thought.

"Did you see those silly assholes in their pom-pom gear?"

The Little Flower of Jesus had spoken, and I looked down to where she stood below Brandon's shoulder.

"Saint Therese?" I said.

"Well at least it's timely," Muffy answered, nudging her father with an elbow.

"I guess I could have done Bo Peep," Brandon said. "But that's taken."

"True enough," Muffy said. "And with style!"

Brandon pushed against her affectionately, and they both smiled.

"You look great, Chris. Absolutely fantastic."

Her smile was beatific under shining, ecstatic eyes. She'd painted her lids and cheeks with some silver moistener and had glued a few joyful tears to the sides of her nose. She wore a modest white shift. A thin golden halo floated above her head. Her hair hung in two thick braids tied with silver ribbons at her shoulders.

"You're stunning," I said.

"You bet your ass," she said. "At least I know some men who would think so. Maybe one or two will be here?"

"I don't doubt it," I said.

"What about Avery and Hans? Are they here yet?"

I was about to answer when the three Carver brothers appeared behind them on the steps, followed by Rudy Vallee and George Burns and Gracie Allen. I could see a few dozen more, animals, various sports and their flapper ladies, all laughing and talking as they crossed the clay. Some stopped to watch Lyle in his juggling and to gaze up at Cora in her magnificence on Blondie's back.

The brothers were farmers who had lost most everything and had turned to hunting and fishing and the sale of their meager produce at a farm stand out front of their weathered house. They were in their twenties and alone now, both of their parents having died of consumption. They'd painted their cheeks with red circles and had dyed their hair, red, green, and yellow, with food coloring. They were half-hearted clowns, dressed in their conventional farmers' overalls, and they were shy as they approached us. I touched Muffy's hand, then turned from her and her father, and greeted them.

"Christine," Bim said. He was the oldest, and I took his

hand, then reached out to touch the others on their shoulders and ushered all three into the house.

A man carrying a vacuum cleaner approached us as we crossed the sill. It was George Brankowski. He was dressed in a cheap, shiny suit, and I suspected it was the one he'd worn to work in earlier times. He put the cleaner on the floor at our feet, then bent over and unzippered the Hoover's bag and dug around inside.

"Where *is* it?" he said, looking up at us, his brows knit.

Then his eyes brightened as he caught sight of the youngest brother's bib. He struggled to his feet and reached out, touching the boy's suspender straps. When his hand pulled back he was holding up a small clay pot. He blew across its surface, a brief white cloud of some powdery substance, and when it drifted away, pink and white petunias stood up from the pot's soil and green vinca vines spilled over and covered his hand and wrist. He turned then, the pot and flowers disappeared, and lifted his cleaner and set off across the foyer. The brothers stood there, mouths agape and eyes following his back as he moved away. When I turned to watch him he was edging among groups of talkative revelers, careful not to bump into them with his machine.

I smelled a rich woody scent. When I turned the Carver brothers were no longer standing there, but Virgo was, her long neck circled in a stack of silver rings that rose to her chin, above which her dark face held a beautiful smile under the nest of snake braids that seethed up almost a foot above her head.

"They're not all *real*, Christine!"

"We added a few taken from horses."

It was Tallahassee, who had stepped out from behind her. A golden disk dripped down from a diadem at the middle of her sleek forehead. He eyes had been painted into Egyptian ovals that feathered out into colorful butterfly wings at her temples, and a long intricate earring, the figure of a bird holding a squirming snake in its beak, hung from her lobe. They both wore long dresses, abstracted organic shapes in no discernible order in the prints. Queen Victoria stood to their left, her face, above the stiff, ribbed dickey, as snowy white as she had promised.

"I'm Yoruba," Virgo said. "A princess!"

"And I'm one too. Most probably from the Arabian Peninsula," said Tallahassee.

"I'm just a queen," said Bret.

"Where's your father?"

"Right here," he said. "Among these united nations."

He'd been standing to my left, a little behind me, and I hadn't seen him, but now he came into view, Abe Lincoln in frock coat and carefully trimmed beard, a stovepipe finer than the Master Comrade's square on his head. He looked remarkably like the president, tall and somewhat ungainly, yet perfectly at ease in that long ago ingrained pitcher's stance. Now he was waiting for another sign, the one that would signal his famous address.

"But I thought the baseball outfit," I said.

"Too baggy."

"That's right," Bret said. "The queen and the princesses decreed something other."

"Quite a good crowd," Tallahassee said. "Is Muffy here yet?"

"Oh, yes, and her father too," I answered, and turned to look for them.

People stood at the food tables and along the walls. Some sat on chairs and couches in the conversation areas Danker and I had devised. I saw the trout there, beside Herbert Hoover. Wine and highball glasses sparkled under the light of the chandelier, and when I looked up and beyond the crystal, near the top of the broad staircase, I saw a moving shadow. There was laughter and talking, a hum of voices rising in greeting, and beyond, in the dining room turned ballroom, the orchestra was playing "Begin the Beguine," that Cole Porter tune, and I knew the party had gotten underway in earnest. I turned and smiled at the Southpaws, touched each of their bodies and kissed Bret and the sisters, then excused myself and moved among the guests, heading for the stairway's foot to greet Bonnefoy. People stopped me on the way, old Angie Niedercorn dressed as a knight in cardboard armor, Adrian Blunt, the optometrist, a third eye in the middle of his forehead. By the time I reached the newel post, Hans was under the painting of my father's dour visage. He was attempting *yoko aruki*, the stealthy sideways walking I had demonstrated for him, hugging the wall, his hands moving out to the sides, then back to cross over his crotch with each new step. I grinned up at him and saw his eyes crinkle above the black fabric of the ninja mask. I'd lent him the outfit and had shown him a few moves, but the garments hung too loosely on his small frame. Even with the temporary hemming and other alterations he looked more like a small child in mother's dress-up than a shadow warrior.

"I feel it!" he said, when he'd negotiated the last step and was my own height where he stood above me in *hira no kamae*, the receiving posture.

"Can I feel it?" he said, and reached out and rested his palm on my bald head.

"I think it might be good for dancing," I said.

He took his hand away.

"I'm certainly up for that!"

"Where's Avery?"

He pushed the sleeve of the black jacket above his wrist and checked his watch, then looked beyond my head to the door, which stood open to the porch. Guests were still coming in. The sun was settling into a pink glow now beyond the frame. Soon

Danker would be throwing the switch, illuminating the parking area and the tents.

"Well, he should be here now," he said. "I'll go over and wait for him."

He passed silently in his split-toed *tabi*, not exactly wraith-like as he nudged among fairy tale figures, Snow White and a half-contingent of dwarfs, Little Red-Cap and her wolf in his licentious grin. I stepped up on the staircase to the second riser for a better view, then saw the stovepipe of the Master Comrade wobbling in the sea of various headgear on the other side of the room. He was moving from one group to another, stopping to talk and gesture. Beyond him, at a drink table near the wall, I saw the Darlings, both in tights and colorful circus jackets and beaded skull caps. Then I saw a metal tube gleaming in the air above the crowd, and in a moment George Brankowski was beside them, lugging his vacuum cleaner, the hose held like a limp, fat snake above his head. He was pointing with it, toward the ceiling. The Darlings were looking up there, following his gesture. Bob lifted his wine glass as if sighting through it, and Amy stood with her hand on her husband's shoulder in a gesture that seemed a tableau-like prelude to some practiced gymnastic feat. Then I saw the MC's stovepipe again as he turned from his conversation with the trout and joined them. He reached to the table, took up a glass, then raised it above his head and began to flick at its rim with a finger. It was noisy in the room. The band was playing a rousing polka, the sound coming in through the open doorway leading to the ballroom. Yet I saw heads turning, the MC's pinging at some frequency that was getting through. Someone moved to the ballroom doors and closed them, and in just moments it was quiet in the room, only a few coughs and a couple of light laughs punctuating the silence.

The MC had left the table's side and was moving among

the partygoers, grumbling, laughing and urging, his words indistinguishable but effective as he cleared a space near the room's center. I saw the Darlings there and George Brankowski, his vacuum cleaner cradled against his chest, but when I looked toward the open doorway I couldn't find Bonnefoy's dark figure, only the ball rising above the crowd, then sinking. Lyle had entered the room, and I thought I saw Cora's crown below his shoulder as his head dipped a little and he sent the ball up again.

The MC stood in the small cleared space, his coattails dancing as he turned in a slow jerky circle, coughing and sputtering, getting rid of some casual language stuck in his throat. Then he paused and reached up and settled his stovepipe firmly on his head. He seemed unsure of himself, yet poised. Lyle's ball kept bouncing from his pate as he moved closer, the crowd parting for his progress. Cora was completely visible at his side now, her hand holding his. She looked up at him when he spoke, his words clear in the hushed room.

"G.E.!" he called out. "IBM!"

"That's right!" the MC said in response. "The acronyms! Utilities and the Union Pacific Railroad. All the buttons and little switches. Why shouldn't the American people take half my money from me? the tycoon asks, I took all of it from them. Retail! On credit! Advertised! What was it the Radio Priest said? I've seen his Little Flower of Jesus in this crowd."

"Christ's Deal!" Lyle said.

"That's right! The New Deal! Roosevelt or ruin! But now he's changed his tune."

"Because the Commies are coming!"

"Or Adolf Hitler, or the Jews, or Benito Mussolini. So much for Christ and *his* deal, the light of social justice. So much for taxes."

George Brankowski held the tube of his vacuum cleaner

hose aloft, the metal attachment at its end shaking above his head. He was attempting some magic, his eyes squinting in concentration as he looked up. Lyle had reached the open space and joined the others. He jerked his head and sent the ball higher. I saw Cora look up and followed her gaze to where the ball settled for a moment, spinning beside the high chandelier before descending. There was a dead bulb there among the others, a flaw of symmetry, and it seem to take on a significance as we all spotted it.

"Well, now you see it," the Master Comrade said. "And there's no forgetting it. We could bring on the ladder?"

"No way!" Lyle called out. "This is our party!"

"Never better said," the MC responded. "Our party. And the light can be a symbol."

"Of social justice?" Cora asked tentatively.

"And union membership?" asked Lyle.

"Absolutely right! They're the same! So long as we can find a way to get it burning again. The go ahead. To get *that* burning. 'The Red Decade,' as the man said."

A light bulb had materialized in George Brankowski's hand. His vacuum cleaner now rested on the floor. We'd been watching the ball's ascension, the MC and Lyle, and now George was looking around, perplexed, the bulb held up in his finger tips, searching for a place to screw it in. It was a frosted bulb, red in color, and slightly larger than the others glowing in the chandelier above. Then the Darlings took center stage, the others moving back slightly, all but George Brankowski, who extended his hand, the bulb held high, and offered it to Bob and Amy, though neither seemed ready to accept it just yet.

It was Bob who did the squatting down this time, Amy facing him, her fingertips on his shoulder as she stepped into the stir-rup cup formed by his hands. Some private communication passed between them, both flexing certain muscles, and in moments they were ready. Amy looked up then and nodded, and George Brankowski extended his arm, offering the light bulb, which Amy accepted as if it were food between her opening lips. George stepped back and fell into a slight crouch, his arms extended toward the Darlings, and I heard a voice at my shoulder, "Chris?" But I didn't turn in response. George's fingers were waving. I heard Bob grunting, then a collective intake of breath as the bulb lit up in Amy's mouth, bathing her face in a red glow. She spoke then, what might have been words garbled into some professional signal as they rumbled out around the bulb stem.

Then Bob rose up like a piston, and Amy was in the air, the beginning of a rocket's ascension, arms at her side and slowly rotating, casting the light in a climbing circle as she shot up toward the high ceiling, where she paused momentarily, her chest at a level with the chandelier. Then she began to fall, and her arms came out at her sides. When they were above her head she grabbed at the matrix of metal and glass and was hanging there and swaying. When the fixture and her body had settled, she released one hand and reached in among the bulbs and unscrewed the dead one, letting it drop immediately. Our eyes followed it down to where it was taken into Lyle's juggling, the bulb and his baseball cap, and the wooden horse and a some small cleaning fixture from George Brankowski's vacuum cleaner. The ball rose a last time, pinging up from his forehead, and when it fell, Cora caught it and held it between her palms and curtsied.

I heard "Chris?" again, and when I turned I was looking down into the face of a woman with red hair, a wig set slightly askew where it cut across her broad brow.

"It's me!" her voice said, and when I glanced to her side, I saw the ninja Bonnefoy, his eyes crinkling above his black mask.

"Avery?" I said.

"The *new* Avery," Bonnefoy answered.

191

A collective exclamation from the crowd then, as if all had discovered the new Avery, and when we looked up again Amy was falling from the chandelier where the red bulb burned brightly among the others.

Her arms were stiff at her sides, her legs together, toes pointed, and when her scull cap detached itself from her head and fell too we knew it would be taken into Lyle's juggling when it reached that circling matrix. Then Bob stepped forward, looking up and bracing himself, and when Amy landed in his arms, he staggered only briefly, then turned with her, held up like a bride ready for the threshold, before he tossed her again and she landed on her feet at his side. They were holding hands now. They both bent at the waist in a deep bow, then turned and bowed again and again, acknowledging the rising applause and calls of "Bravo" and "Brava" that came from all quarters of the room.

→NINETEEN←

Dusk had settled in the junipers that formed the maze, muffled voices from there, sharp laughter and sexual giggles. It was nine o'clock, but the solstice, and darkness was slow in coming.

A fresh contingent of guests had arrived in the last hour, high school friends and acquaintances dressed elaborately as dead and aged faculty, police and other town officials from that time Muffy and I had shared with them. They made the past live again, but insanely. They'd been visiting the bars. Many among them were drunk and staggering by the time they came, passing the Lipper twins, who shied away from them on their way out. Others too, Andy Brownbear and his four sisters, and even his father, all costumed as Ghost Dance visions in feathers, beads, and frightening masks. We could hear the band playing in the distance, a Charleston soaked in nostalgia for those of the proper age. Some were under the tents beyond the porch, their shoulders hunched over the food tables, and we could hear a crunching of chicken bones, groans, and lips smacking.

"They're hungry," Muffy said.

She sat in the shadows cast by the porch eaves, her elbows on the table. Her face was luminous even in the darkness, as if the shine of ecstasy were coming from her soul, which was the idea of her costume after all. I could see the tear pearls on her cheeks, never falling.

"Well, it's a party," her father said.

He'd taken to punctuating his talk with the pistol. He must have reloaded from time to time; smoke drifted from the barrel whenever he waved it. The blood remained vivid at his temple.

"I mean *hungry*," Muffy said. "Literally. Didn't you see the way they crowded around the tables? It's a reminder. It's a good thing that we see it."

"I saw it," I said.

"That Master Comrade," she said. "He's a real pisser. What he says? It's funny, but it's serious too."

"That's right," her father said. "Bring on the revolution. That kind of thing."

"And what about our Avery?" I said.

"Oh, shit!" Muffy laughed. "Now we're talking!"

Avery's was the most dramatic costume at the party, because it was absolutely clear that it was Avery Brattle under the clothing. He wore wedgies and bobby socks and above that a pleated wool skirt that ended just below the knees. His blouse was of the peasant style, billowing sleeves and deep at the cleavage between his prominent falsies. Great care had been taken with his makeup, and surely he'd been practicing his walk, that twitch of the hips, and the hand gestures that rattled the bracelets at his wrists. The band had played a slow tango. He and the ninja Bonnefoy had taken center stage, that small dark figure flowing across the floor in the arms of a large school girl, though it was the ninja who was leading, dipping and twirling Avery at just the right moments. They'd been to Chicago for things other than business. "Lessons in the art," Bonnefoy had told me. Though they were a strange vision as they turned and jerked their heads from side to side, they danced with a practiced grace.

Almost everyone at the party knew Avery Brattle, and though he laughed with them when they commented upon his dress, there was a steady look in his eye that centered him below his shyness. Avery dressed up as anything at all, given his fragile dignity, would have been something to watch and consider, but this went deeper than that, this display of himself as another. I think we all wondered if it was now possible for him to return to that Avery we had all known. Maybe *that* was the costume.

"I suspect they'll be settling their business soon," Muffy said dryly.

"Looks like some fucking monkey-business to me," said her father, waving his pistol between us. It had grown dark on the porch, and we could no longer see smoke at the barrel.

George Brankowski was sitting beside Cora in the breakfast nook where Danker and I took most of our morning meals, when I entered the kitchen, then made my way among the white figures working at the sinks and stoves. Cora's crown had tilted to the side and seemed ready to fall as she leaned over to suck Coke through a straw. George was sipping coffee, his vacuum on the floor beside him. He lifted the cup when he saw me. I'd been traveling through the party in my bones for the last hour, and I could feel the sweat on my brow and above my ears. He saw it and pulled a napkin from the holder and handed it to me as I sat down across from them.

I'd circled the parking area, Muffy and her father strolling with me, had greeted some guests and checked to be sure there was enough food still at the tables. We'd avoided the maze, but could hear the revelers as they smooched and did God knows what in the various cul-de-sacs. I'd left Muffy and Brandon under a tent. The Carver brothers were there, and Muffy kissed each one of them, her ecstatic lips pressed to clown cheeks. The brothers' plates were full, and they were eating slowly, savoring each mouthful. Brandon had holstered his pistol in his belt, then lifted plates for his daughter and himself. The five stood in a loose circle, eating and talking quietly.

Things were somewhat subdued in the entrance hall. The guests had eaten enough to take the edge off appetite and only a few were at the tables. The rest stood in clusters under paintings near the walls or sat in chairs and couches, glasses in their hands or on the coffee tables Danker had placed there. The Champagne buckets had been replenished with fresh bottles. I saw that there was plenty of wine, liquor and ice. The hired crew was doing a proper job, but where was Danker? Then I saw him come out of my father's study in his monk's robe. He too was checking. He raised his hand and smiled in greeting from across the room.

In the dining room turned dancehall things were different. The place was packed, and though Danker had opened the windows and the curtains lifted in a light breeze, smoke hung in the air and people were dancing in it, some costumes in disarray. The cheerleaders seemed real in their sweat now, enthusiastic at the victory party after the game. Even the trout was fresh from water. Herbert Hoover seemed properly beleaguered as he turned in the arms of Eleanor Roosevelt. The band was playing a slow fox trot, a respite for lovers following the energy of a half dozen polkas. I saw Avery and Bonnefoy sprawled in a couch beside the Darlings.

"You've been dancing," I said.

I had to speak loudly over the tone of the trumpet that was taking a pure, unfiligreed solo, liquid and seductive. Amy Darling smiled up at me and grunted something. "Oop!" Bob Darling said in agreement, or something like that.

"Were you here for Norma Lipper? You should have seen that!"

It was Avery, his familiar voice coming from that unfamiliar face. I stared hard at him, my own face guarded from any clear reading under my paint. I could find the old Avery there easily, his look, but not this bold-eyed freedom of expression.

"She played the saxophone," Bonnefoy said.

He'd unhooked the black veil and was himself even in this ludicrous costume he'd come to wear with considerable grace. Now he looked like some sheik in a harem.

"*Played* it? She set it on fire!"

Avery's red wig vibrated as he laughed and gestured broadly with hands and arms, his bracelets clacking and shimmering at his wrists. Hans watched him, a look both quizzical and fond as he pursed his lips prior to grinning. The fox trot came to a long and languorous ending, and after applause, the high hat tapped out the beginning rhythm of a samba. I saw Bonnefoy's extended hand as he rose up flowing in his black garments, then Avery's, limp wristed, his nails painted glossy red. The ninja assumed a version of *hira no kamae*, the receiving posture, having to lean back a bit in his effort to pull the heavier man up from the couch. When he did come up he was turning, his hand elevated, grasping the other, which he pirouetted under. Then that unlikely couple drifted onto the dance floor in small and gracefully mincing steps.

I took the napkin George Brankowski offered, pressed it against my brow and wiped my entire head with it. It came away wet and sticky. He had another ready and I used that too. Both he and Cora looked like tired puppies.

"A little sick of magic," George said, and I heard the Coke bubbling as Cora breathed out through the straw.

Her crown was almost to the side of her head now, held there in her gnarled and sweaty hair. I reached across the table, meaning to right it.

"It's okay," she said. "I want to go to sleep now."

"Me too," George said. "In a little while at least."

"Where's Lyle?" I said. "I haven't seen him."

"In bed," Cora said.

It was after eleven now and many of the older folks had departed, leaving the party to those under fifty, who in their drink and costumes felt much younger than that. Those who *were* younger paced themselves, dancing only the slow tunes, aware of their limits and tomorrow's retribution.

"Why don't you go?" I said. "To bed, I mean."

"I can't get undressed," Cora said. "I ate too much."

Her crown was close to her ear and she was looking across the table, searching for the face of the woman she'd gone fishing with, finding it as her eyes brightened, then losing it again in tiredness. Her words were a plea, a little coy and testing, and I rose up to it, wanting what I thought she wanted. George, even in his own exhaustion, saw this pass between us, subtle as it was, and responded with an equal subtlety, though quite directly.

"I'll hold down the fort," he said. "See ya in the morning."

This was the cue for our rising. I held Cora's plump hand as we made our way through the dark passage behind the kitchen, heading for the servants' quarters.

She was right about the clothing, but not the cause. The crinoline had stiffened at her collar and across her chest. Clasps and buttons, dormant since my own childhood, were caught up now in fabric and rusted metal. I had to struggle to loosen her binding, even clip a few hairs away in order to free the crown. She was compliant, turning her body and lifting her head to look at me, stoically, as I worked to undress her.

We sat beside each other on the bed. She had her own small room with a bath attached, and near the door of the bathroom the boxes I'd brought down from the attic were carefully stacked. There were four of them, all bulging with my childhood clothing. I wondered at the fact that I'd brought down so much. The need had been for night clothes and hiking gear, no more than that, but I'd carried down other things, both dress-up and casual.

"I don't like it," she said, once she was free of her costume and was sitting with her legs dangling down at the bed's side in her tattered underwear. I'd gone to the bathroom to wet a wash cloth and get the brush from the old shell set I'd given her and was coming out through the doorway when she spoke.

"The things I brought you?" I asked, a little startled by her comment as I crossed the room and sat down beside her again. I lifted her chin in my fingers and began washing away the makeup.

"No," she said. "Your bones."

"It's only a costume," I said.

"No it isn't," she said insistently, looking up at me and turning her face as I scrubbed lightly at her cheeks and the liner I'd darkened her brows with. "You're not dead!"

"Well, of course not," I said, startled again.

"But you're dressed up that way."

I had no answer for that.

When the makeup was gone, I took the pins from her tresses, worked at the gnarled strands with my fingers, then lifted the brush, her hair on my palm, and began stroking through it. It grew fine as any child's hair as it disentangled, the sheen coming back, raven as my own had been when I'd had it.

"Do you miss your breasts?" she said, the question so quiet and sincere and intimate that I answered it immediately.

"Yes," I said. "I guess at times I do. Maybe just the weight and the feel in clothing. But not all the time."

"Amy showed me hers," she said. "They hang down."

"That's because she's getting old. It's natural."

"Mine won't."

"No," I said. "They'll come right out. High and nice."

"Milk?" she said.

"Well, that's when you get pregnant. Milk for the baby? It won't come before that."

"I know *that*!" she said. "But do you miss it? That, and your hair too?"

"I've never had a need for it. No babies here." I touched my stomach through the bony girdle of my costume. "As for the hair? I kind of like this. No brushing and fussing necessary anymore."

"I like it too," she said, her head back in pleasure now in the brushing. I wondered if anyone had ever tended to her in this way. Maybe Amy Darling had, her mother in a time she couldn't quite remember. Surely no one else. Nor had I been active in such tending, liking it just as much as she did.

We went into the bathroom together. She was slightly slumping, and she raised her arms in a way that seemed practiced, though I knew it wasn't that but only natural in her trust, and I pulled her half slip over her head, then stood there as she pulled her panties down and let them fall around her ankles, a pool of soiled fabric she stepped out of as I held her elbow.

She was white, smooth chested and hairless, and I stood to the side and looked down at her as she brushed her teeth, then wet a wash cloth and wiped under her arms and between her legs, gestures that I thought of as pathetic, lost child gestures, pragmatic on-the-road efficiencies. Yet they *were* efficient and suggested a certain wherewithal beyond her age. I wondered how many other children had found themselves in a fix similar to hers and guessed hundreds, maybe even thousands. I thought I might be looking into the very heart of this long Depression, children returned to a time when they were thought of as less than developed humans, only wild things, and as such had been forced into their adult humanity and the self-reliance necessary for survival in such a world.

When she was finished, she turned and looked up at me. Then she moved against me, her arms encircling my hips and her head against my stomach. I put my hand over her ear, under the freshly brushed hair, and pulled her tight against me.

"You can't see the bones now," I whispered.

"You're warm," she said, her words muffled, tickling slightly where her mouth pressed into my belly.

I led her back into the room then, and she sat naked on the bed's side, on the sheet above the turned down covers, as I went to the boxes near the door and fished around in one of them. I was looking for the nightshirt, the favorite I'd worn in those years before any care, and I found it almost immediately. Strangely, it felt fresh in my fingers, and when I raised the flannel and pressed my face into it, the only scent was the sweet one of a distant childhood, very faint in the fabric and most probably only imagined.

Her arms were already lifted by the time I reached her, and the gown fell loosely over her body and seemed to fit perfectly. I adjusted the fabric at her shoulders, then leaned over and pushed her gently, watching her plump legs as she slipped her feet below the covers. Then I lifted the covers and tucked them around her. Her head was on the pillow, her dark hair a halo on the white fabric, and she was smiling up at me, her lids already falling. Still, she was waiting, ready for the last term of our engagement, the one that would send her, formally, into untroubled sleep.

"Dear little Cora," I whispered, then leaned over and touched her brow and kissed her on the lips. "Sweet dreams."

I went down the back hallway and into the kitchen again, where I lingered, holding the words I'd passed with Cora as they had been, before they became a lesson, or psychological, or a fable, their feel crumbling away as they joined the logic of memory. It was late now, time closing in on the first hour of the new day, and I was tired and ready for a quiet moment before the party began to wind down to its last goodbyes.

George Brankowski was gone, his coffee cup still on the kitchenette table, and the people in white were still busy, though moving soporifically. It was mostly drink, trays of Champagne and highballs carried out and among the remaining revelers. Dirty dishes filled the counter and a man was working at them with a brush in the sudsy sink. I took a glass from a passing tray. When I sipped it I knew what I really wanted was the meerschaum and some solitude. I stepped out of the kitchen and made my way into the foyer, where only a few costumed figures lingered on the couches and loveseats, some deep in conversation, others with their heads back on the cushions, resting. I looked up at the hanging crystal and saw the red bulb, magical among the white. I could hear music faintly from beyond the closed ballroom doors, a slow tune. The orchestra was winding down to the last dance, traditional, farewell to the party and its artifice.

The study was dark, but the dim lights under the tent canopies beyond the window illuminated the desk surface and the table lamp upon it. I made my way around at the corner and sat down in my father's chair, then retrieved the pipe and tobacco and a box of matches from the drawer. I was packing the bowl when I felt a presence in the shadows.

"Do you feel that?" a voice whispered.

It was the Master Comrade. When I squinted I could see the shape of his stovepipe hat where it rested like a squatting animal on the seat of a wing chair near the wall. The shadow of his small figure stood beside it.

"Come into the light," I said, turning the desk lamp switch even as I spoke.

"I didn't mean," he said. "To startle you, I mean."

He moved up out of the darkness, leaving his hat behind. I gestured toward the leather easy chair in which my father had located those he had serious business with.

"You're hiding out?"

"No. Not that," he said.

He held a drink in his hand, a tall tumbler half-full of some clear liquid, which he raised up and stared at as if he'd just discovered it there.

"I guess it's water," he said. "The ice seems to have melted. I was looking at your father's books."

He wasn't performing now. The usual animation in his face had given way to age lines and a puffiness below the eyes. I could see he was older than I'd thought previously.

"In the dark?"

"Oh, no. It's not dark over there. Once the eyes are accustomed. It's a curious library, handy for the use of it, but nothing at all to do with business, or even trees, which I take it was the material world behind it."

"And oil," I said. "A few leases anyway."

"Ah, yes. Petroleum. Petrol, and the natural gas. That, together with steel and wood. They build and power the world. There's stone, of course, and brick."

"And water," I said. "Do you think we'll be coming out of this world soon?"

"Oh absolutely! Just a few more years. There's war on the

horizon. That always improves things. Though not some other things. And already the unions are back and very strong again. It won't be long at all."

"It's been a hell of a century."

"So far," he said. "Perhaps the bitter half. Then it's sunlight on the emblems, those amber reeds of grain."

"Waves," I said. "But I wouldn't count on it."

"Of course. But it's the lingo. Glory's road, you know."

I'd tamped the meerschaum, then struck a match and lit it, the Cuban tobacco sweet and soothing in my nose. I leaned back in the chair and watched him. He'd spread his coattails primly before sitting, and his thick hair, though still a bit matted from the hat, was edging out again into a bushy corona. His face was drawn, but his eyes sparkled in the dimness beyond the desk light's reach. I could hear the distant sounds of the instruments, the party limping along, and I wondered if Bonnefoy and Avery were dancing a waltz this time.

"And what's to become of you," I said, "and your troupe?"

He didn't hesitate.

"That's a question. But not a problem. This is really a holding action. A little experiment in communal living. We'll stay together until there's no more need for that. Then we'll go our separate ways."

"What about the children?"

"Time will take its course. But what about yours?"

"My what?" I said.

"*Your* holding action."

He was looking at my head. Then he lowered his eyes to the bones, the sternum and the ribs.

"I don't know," I said. "It's cancer of course. I can't be making any plans."

"Of course you can. That's exactly what you can do. Unlike

most of us. All but the very old, which it seems I'm getting to be. You can decide upon distribution, can't you? Plans on paper, but only to spend time being morbid, if that's what you like. But you could take a motor trip with Muffy, make plans for that. She's got a very fine car. All the best plans are short-term anyway. Keeping in touch with the present? The possibilities are endless, if you can figure out what you want."

"You met her?" I asked.

"Fuck yes," he said, smiling. "To put it in the right language."

"Lyle should be calling out at this time."

He laughed at that. "Something about a parody of the polyterritans?"

"That's right," I said. "The Red Decade."

"Were that it was."

"Are you serious about all that?"

"In a way," he said. "I'm serious about responsibility, these skills that went down to nothing in the crash. I'm the organization man, born again. You might say that. The returns are short term now, but they're real and not paper."

"And what was the commodity?" I asked.

"Paper," he said. "Futures. Not even dollar bills."

"So it was the Market then. But how did you come to that pass? Where did it start from?"

He looked away for a moment, reaching back to something, an odd smile upon his face. Then he looked back at me, hesitant it seemed, but still smiling.

"You're asking for a long story," he said. "And mostly a useless thing. But I do remember a bit of one. Would you like to hear it?"

"Go on," I said.

But he didn't. Not right away. First he lifted his glass and sipped from it, then reached down beside the chair and rested it on the carpet. It was quiet in the room as he shifted in his seat. I found I couldn't hear the music in the distance anymore. Then he pulled a large white handkerchief from his coat pocket and blew his nose sedately, then folded it and wiped his brow with it. The handkerchief was in his hands then on his stomach and he was talking.

"My father once knew a man named Johnny Teeth. Before that, back in a misty time before I was sentient and knew anyone, he had been called Johnny Talk because he talked too much.

"My father was a carpenter, a gun smith by hobby, and a cabinet maker, and my mother was a charismatic Catholic, somewhat special in the Mississippi Delta at that time. Her conversion to my father's faith, which he'd abandoned, gave her the accoutrements she'd missed in her Baptist system of belief. She had her altars and candles now, her rosaries and holy cards, and those children's picture books, *Lives of the Saints*, she read and gazed at rapturously, easily moved by their redemptive plight and joyful weeping.

"We're talking about eighteen-eighty-six here, horses drawing wagons in the Delta mud, and Johnny Teeth among my father's cronies in his small shop behind the house, not working, but drinking, and I'm among them and just fifteen years old. It's early afternoon, a dark sky in the rain, and I can see the shapes of sodden horses through the window. Candles stand in a wax pool on a barrel, and somebody's asking Johnny Teeth for information, a story, some bit of local history, his political positions, anything that will get him going, but Johnny Teeth isn't talking, though he's having a hard time of it. This is what happened.

"Johnny Talk had been talking for as long as anyone could remember. There was no conversation when he was around, unless it was fought for, and the battles were exhausting. Even victory amounted to very little, brief comments that would seem to stand alone, only to fall invariably, like kindling, into the fire of his monologue, becoming its fuel. He could talk about anything, and could do it in a way that was elegant, like politicians can, so that knowledge and information had nothing to do with it. Thus no subject, however arcane, would forestall him. God knows they looked for one—the fur trade in Alaska, secrets of the secret brotherhood of the Freemasons, embalming techniques—but they had no successes, and in a while they gave up on that approach and tried insult and even physical abuse, shoulder punches and whacks on the back that were much harder than good fellowship warranted.

"Though these actions relieved their rage and frustration momentarily, they had no lasting effect on Johnny Talk and the vacuous hypnotism of his talking, which came often in the form of stories. Seldom did he speak of his own life in them, only at times as prologue to get into them, but this is exactly what the others were missing, that placement of themselves in a meaningful narrative, and because of this some wished to kill him, to finally silence him, but even these wondered about a future without him, not sure at all what they might talk about then, dimly recognizing the utter boredom that was the real and only subject matter of their lives.

"Then one day the Slacket brothers came around, Asterid and Kyle, their names as sneaky and evil as the little bastards they were and remained even in their old age, when I came to know and despise them as much as my father and the others did. Johnny Talk had fallen victim to bilateral toothache, one in a molar on each side, and wasn't talking. When the brothers arrived and discovered his malady, they were solicitous and sweet and helpful in their sneakiness. They spoke of someone they knew who was a very good dentist and even offered to deliver Johnny Talk into his company for relief, which they did, taking him away with them in their wagon. But the dentist was their relative and had the same ethics, and at the brothers' instructions he performed a strange dental surgery. He drilled out the molars, then lined the new cavities with steel. Then he inserted small metal balls into those spaces before sealing them over for good and all.

"After the surgery, Johnny Talk quit talking for a long while, until he could manage the new sound and motion. Only then was he able to explain the reason behind his reticence, such explanation incumbent upon him, since the others had been urging him ever since he fell silent, having nothing at all to talk about but that. And when he did speak he became know from then on as Johnny Teeth.

"The balls rocking and clicking against each other in his mouth set up a vibration there and in his entire head, and this was apparent even when he breathed deeply, though far more dramatic in effect when he spoke, even a few words. 'Let's see now' became a pointed and assured prologue to important things to follow, the correction of some flawed logic or the beginning of knowledgeable discourse, "Let us now see the correct lay of the land." His head became a megaphone, as if he were at a podium, and every word spoken gathered weight and distinction even as his teeth did, each of which seemed to step forward individually and to swell out together like some orchestra peopled by many primadonnas.

"Outside his mouth, his words were now heard followed by an almost imperceptible echo, just enough to transmit a hint of what he felt inside and to gather up his audience's attention in a way unknown to them before. They now needed to listen to what he was saying, rather than to be figuring ways to interrupt the flow with their own local egos. This was difficult all around, but more for Johnny Teeth than the others. He mastered the new mechanics early on, but it took a long while for him to come back to dominance. They were listening to his words now, and there seemed two ways to go. He could remain self-conscious, but a manipulator of this new stage and his listeners, or he could find a way to forget about it all, become relaxed and sincere as he had been before and just get back to the pleasures of the talking, though he knew he'd always need their urging now before beginning because of his lingering discomfort in this new role as one whose words were attended to.

"He chose the latter course. It was the harder of the two, but it was the only way to avoid masquerade. These were his friends, and he did not wish his words to be a barrier between himself and them. In a while, he was able to explain this to them, though awkwardly and with a feeling of great distaste because the explanation was about nothing other than himself. They might have understood his dilemma and its solution, at least I think my father did, for this is how he told it to me, one night while we were at the table awaiting dinner, my mother praying over her cooking, those plaster figures and up-ended holy cards on a shelf above the stove.

"And so we're back in the shed again, and it's warm there and raining, and my father and the others are drinking, but they're working too, trying to get Johnny Teeth going. Somebody tells a brief story, local and about themselves as the hero of some insignificant bargaining for a horse or halter, and Johnny Teeth is listening to the story attentively. Then, finally, he clears his throat, a slight echo in the air in the cozy space, and says, *And that reminds me of a time when Asterid Slacket worked at the Feed and Grain and was stealing whatever he could find at hand because it was his nature and everyone knew about that and it became a story and part of the public wheel, said public defined only by those who know such stories, the ones named by outsiders as local knowledge, incorrect as this is even now, and will become even more wrong-headed when technology takes over in future time.*

But at this time, the owner knew of the stealing and tallied all of it, adding hours and subtracting from Slacket's cash payments weekly to cover it: thus an economic system, Slacket humanized through the pleasure of his stealing on the job, the owner receiving his just dues.

But what is justice? This story? But it was facts quickly organized to become others, perverted into acceptability by being given an easy enough narrative and its simplistic punch line, like the exaggerated death toll of an earthquake in Ecuador. Where exactly is Ecuador, what does it look like, could its people find a way to express their feelings to us? Who cares? Such a story is the safety of ourselves, realized in disaster at a distance, and that's a much better story than Asterid Slacket's thievery, which hardly anyone remembers anymore.

Big times are ahead. The efficiency of the U.S. Mail system is ahead. You'll be able to get a letter from Ecuador in just a few days. Local stories will fall under the weight of the news from distant places, our own Washington, but gay Paris and London too. And who exactly will we be then, still sitting in this shed, telling stories about men like Slacket and ourselves, even in a voice that has the authority of a megaphone, though it call out from an empty field of play? It's okay that time passes, but to pass us by? Yet it's too late to be younger, wanderers, to have our own stories come back foreign and exotic to this place.

It sounds utterly depressing, doesn't it? Sounds quite impossible. Maybe we should just lay down and die, or get religion, or lie about our importance in some story designed only to display that. Or we could get cracker-barrel philosophical: "so long as I got my health and clean underwear," become the old fools we may well be already. I don't know. The thing may be to just keep talking, now that our future is in the past, not to talk about that anymore, but to tell expanded stories, forget ourselves and Slacket altogether, stories like reading a newspaper come across the seas. We could have the whole world that way and get a little younger as we get old.

That's the proposal, and even as I voice it I think of something else, a story that goes beyond this place, and the thinking that goes before the telling is much like reading, or remembering, a tale inside a foreign book. It's not the Good Book or those other ones that stand in opposition to it, but it will have to do. It's good enough for the Mississippi Delta after all, and good enough for us too.

⇥TWENTY⇤

From the moment I set foot in the twentieth century I felt fragile and alone. I was among those I thought I'd come to know and even cherish, but from the distance of a wealthy woman who could crawl into her comfortable bed at night and drift into that welcome oblivion free of significant care. Now I was among them, though not of them, and could scent their individual desperations in sweat under piped-in deodorants, could hear and see it in fitful snoring and the way bodies lurched, shifting in sleep's fractured narratives.

It was the night train become a milk train, scheduled from Chicago to Philadelphia and New York City with many stops between. It had its source in Los Angeles, its cargo a company that changed its configurations at cities and whistle-stops across the country, together commonly in that each headed for promise and away from the loss of it. These were not the completely downtrodden and resigned who had found community of plight, but those who could still imagine hope, if only vaguely, and the inherent American competition that came with it and thus isolated each.

I'd been informed at the counter. The Pullman sleeper I'd reserved was not available, nor was the Twentieth Century Limited itself. There was only the All-Coach, just a few seats left. I could wait until the following day. They'd put me up at some hotel and would straighten things out. But I had appointments, and though it would be a twenty-hour trip, I could sleep, so I took what was left, then searched for a porter and could not find one. I was traveling much lighter than usual, so I lugged my suitcase up and found my seat among them, a window seat, the one on the aisle empty until a thin young man in a worn and rumpled suit sat down beside me and I could smell the cheap liquor on his breath. Then the train was lumbering from the station, past the stock yards, headed for South Bend. I turned away from the man and looked into the dark window. I could hear a child whimper, its coughing through hot tears and acrid cigarette smoke just a few rows ahead below dirty night lights, and in that overheated coach, as if a boxcar headed for uncertain fortune, I could feel the gum melting into a sticky sap under my wig.

What wanderlust remained in the troupe members melted away when the Master Comrade suggested they decamp and travel to fresh fields. Their hesitancy was quickly read by him. The children, after all, could use permanence of place and education, I argued. He'd nodded in quick agreement, pointing out the good qualities of my library and noting that both he and the Darlings, especially Amy, could set up their lessons on a regular basis. George Brankowski was mad for the cleaning and before I left was removing the storm windows. Soon he would begin the task of washing all the windows in the house, and then, he said with a bright gleam in his eyes, it would be time to get after the third floor, those many rooms that had been closed up tight for years. Count Southpaw's garden and orchard were coming into bud and first vegetables. I'd seen him plotting with Amy and Bob. Danker told me of their extravagant plans. They would reconnoiter the acreage, plant trees, clear away deadfall, get the entire place in shape. And Lyle was fishing and trapping, Bret was cooking his catch, and Cora was grooming Blondie and Young Lyle, reading and working to learn sewing under the tutelage of Virgo and Tallahassee. And I was loathe to leave all this and take up the masquerade of my profession yet again.

At Toledo the young man struggled to his feet, half-drunk now and shrunken into that dimension depressively, and dragged his small cardboard suitcase from the rack above. I saw its checkered side as he set it on the empty seat, then adjusted his clothing and hair. Someone was meeting him, or maybe the case was a sales case of some kind and he was heading for business that would not materialize. I watched him weave down the aisle, stepping over boxes and bags full of clothing and children's battered toys that blocked the way. Then I turned again to the window and saw the others waiting on the platform under the dim lights in a hot rain. They were not begging. Some were handsome in their reserve, their faces only mildly expectant as they searched for faces in the crowd that staggered from the train, some carrying children and bundles, to find themselves greeted with a few tears and handshakes.

It was close to midnight and dark in the rain. I saw a man selling mealy apples carried in a frayed wicker basket, then saw the young man with the cardboard suitcase pass beside him to be swallowed up in the crowd. There were children looking to shine shoes in the rain and a woman calling out a plea to Moses, or Jesus, or Roosevelt, her voice faintly audible through the window. There were men who wore women's coats that had been cast away, who held pieces of cardboard over their heads in the rain, and women in men's shirts and trousers, one whose hair had been viciously shorn to reveal scabs at her temple. A boy tripped drunkenly in rags tied round his ankles in place of shoes, and a woman held up a child tucked in a pillow case, offering it. She was weeping, and another woman, much younger, pulled desperately at her sleeve. They all seemed to be sliding together on the platform back to where the train had come from, but it was the train that was moving.

They were gone then, and I turned from the window. An older man, smelling of sweat and garlic, was lowering himself into the vacant seat. Again I turned, city lights flickering beyond the frame now, and attempted sleep, but it would not come. The coach lurched at the switches, moving slowly as it left the city, then continued that way over rails needing repair. Newspapers rustled under a few night lights, and children wept quietly in exhaustion. Adult groans and whimpers punctuated the constant drone.

At the solstice party, no one had seemed surprised when they saw my bald head and the absence of my breasts, and I was now quite sure that my condition had been revealed to all while I was still in the hospital recovering. I mistrusted no one, though I knew it would have been hard for Muffy, all that commerce at her candy shop. Still, it was most probably leaked from the hospital itself, or by the doctors at some party or dinner. My father had been well known in Minneapolis and I, as his daughter, was known there too. Once the news found its way to Hayward there would have been no stopping it.

At the party I had dressed both for concealment and revelation, but I saw now that what I had accomplished was only display. I'd spoken to no one about this, and that was concealment, but when I learned from Bret that she and the Count and her nieces had known of my consultation disguises all along, I was taken into a world quite different from the one where I thought I lived. I figured I had to begin some questioning of my machinations, though Bret had forestalled such thoughts immediately. "Christine," she'd said. "It makes no difference. We all thought it made perfect sense. We know about such things, if you'll allow me, being black negroes. You're a woman after all." And that brought me back to a centering once again and to a realization of the utter distaste of both my profession and the costumes it required.

And so I knew I was packing to enter into this public role for the last time and, not wanting to count on eccentricity or the theatrical, had left the diamond stud behind, as well as any outrageous garb that in the past had made too much of a game out of these consults. I'd packed only plain clothing, slacks, ties and jackets, and had dressed in grey twill pants and a dark green cotton shirt for the train ride. My wig had been fashioned in Chicago, at the best place available, and I had an odd revelation when I stood in front of the mirror before leaving. My shirt was much tighter than any I'd worn before, but my breasts were gone now and I needed no billowing to hide them. The wig was quite good. I looked more like a man than I ever had before, and I knew, even if I stripped down to my undershirt and shorts and took the wig off, I might still look like that. A man in a woman, and very little difference at all between them.

I shifted in my seat, sleepless and tired and with a sheen of sweat sticky on my brow, and the man beside me spoke in offering and handed across the greasy paper bag he'd held in his lap.

"It's sausage," he said. "Vegetable, and some pork and garlic. My wife made it. There's a knife in there."

He was wiry and small, a little older than I, but he had plenty of hair, gone grey at the temples, and a heart of gold. It was sewn in over the breast pocket of his cotton jacket. He saw me noting it as I accepted the offering.

"My wife. She's good at sewing," he said.

"What about children?" I asked. "Do you have any?"

"Oh, yes. A half-dozen. The boys are off on the rails though. We get cards. There's bread down in there too."

I cut a plug of sausage and tore at the crusty bread at the bag's bottom. It was warm on my fingers, a dense yet airy loaf. Then I made a little sandwich and held it up before tasting.

"Your wife," I said.

"That's right. She bakes good bread as well."

"Is that in Toledo?"

"Graytown," he said. "A few miles from there. I'm heading for New York City, to the patent office. Then a few buyers. I'm doing inventions now."

He raised his hands to the edge of some enthusiasm. Then they fell to the bag I'd handed back to him. His knuckles were torn and calloused, his cuffs frayed.

"Must be a hard row to hoe, in this day and age."

"Not much that isn't," he said. "But maybe this time. They're traps, animal traps. They don't kill the animals."

I wondered about the sausage for a moment. I could smell dead animals in the coach, a stew of scavenged foods or fatty leavings bought cheaply then prepared to hide lack of quality: fried chicken backs, bean chilies laced with pork rind, the brains of diseased coons caught in the wild.

"Is this your first one?" I asked.

"Oh, no," he said. "There've been a few others, since I lost the work. Nothing to speak of. What do you do?"

He'd been forthcoming, but when he asked the question he turned his eyes away, as if he'd breached the terms of our casual acquaintance. He seemed a good man, one who was hiding his desperation out of a sense of appropriateness.

"I consult at prisons," I said. "About escapes. I help to stop them."

"That's odd," he said. "I mean, I'm trapping and so are you. I wonder where they go, the escapers. Do you ever wonder about that?"

"I do. But what do you think?"

He thought for a moment, one hand patting the bag his wife had sent him off with, to be close to him I fancied. Then he smiled, a tentative smile.

"Well," he said. "With these traps of mine there's a problem. Getting food for bait is a problem, but that's not the one I'm talking about. You hang the food inside. Then when the animal goes for it, a wire door falls down and he's trapped. The problem has been getting them out of there, once they're in there? Seems they don't always want to leave. Many just sit there, waiting for the bait again. It's where the food is and I think shelter too from those who would come to make food of them. I think it may well be the times, that it's gotten down even into the animal world. Isn't that something?

"And I'd think it might be that way too with prisoners, though they are not animals. I'd wonder first just how many who escape are caught and come back again, really because they feel a need to be caught, to get back to food and safety. Does this sound somewhat crazy?"

"Not at all," I said. "It sounds right. Maybe the food is more than just food."

"Like this sack," he said, lifting it from his lap. "My wife, you know."

We sat there in silence for a few moments, both feeling I think that we'd gotten to the heart of things too quickly, that it had to be more complex than we'd come to make it, more subtle than that. His heart of gold shone on his pocket in the night lights, almost pulsing. I didn't know quite where we were. Had we passed by Cleveland yet? No longer were the children whimpering. I could hear snoring, an occasional cough, stertorous breathing. Then the man patted his greasy bag again and began talking.

"There are other traps out there of course, but mine has a few design twists and four entrances. It has the shape of a cross, East, West, North and South, and in the center a chamber where the bait is hung, or hooked up on the floor. The animal enters from one of the four directions, and any touch of the bait is a trigger and all the doors close. The mechanics are very simple, but foolproof. Only a human hand can open the thing up for escape. You could drive or hand-carry the trap to a far distance, then release the animal in the hopes that it won't find a way back. Coons, you know, and red squirrels and the opossum, they can wreak havoc in a house. You've got to take them far away, and even then some are bound to return. Unless it's others. They look very much alike. It's hard to tell.

"I came upon the idea after the World War, when I was working in metallurgy at the steel mill in Toledo, the job I lost, then couldn't find another when the Depression began.

"In the mill they had us in an enclosure, on display, a glass chamber near the plant's center. We wore suits and ties, costumes that distinguished us from the mill workers, as did our place in that glass room. It was clean there and the temperature was constant, both needful conditions for the testing of yield, tensile strength, and elongation. The room was glass so that visitors to the plant, those executives and government politicians, could see in to the careful work we were doing there. That way the mill could instill confidence in them and get better contracts.

"I remember feeling, when people looked in at us, that I was a specimen or an actor on a stage, and that my clothing was a disguise. I was just a young man, back from the war, on-the-job training, then doing that job.

"But that's not the point. It was simply that chamber and its transparency, the trips I'd have to take from various parking lots through corridors in the plant's unfriendly heat to get there, and the strong *desire* to get there, to arrive at respite and safe well-being. This, and some thoughts about the physical configurations involved. That gave me the idea for my trap and its possibilities. But now, as I think of it...

"As I think of it, I remember the war and our travel through byways in a broken landscape to those foxholes, given the name 'graves' at Belleau Wood, where we pissed in our pants and wept for our mothers and home.

"We were dressed as soldiers, had been given an idea of what that meant by men who were also dressed that way and had no idea at all of the realities that lay before us. All were in costume at that time, dressed up as soldiers, but it was masquerade, though our real selves leaked through that clothing with our piss and tears, and we found community beyond any disguise at all in our extremity, but at too high a cost.

"And now this Depression and a high cost too, for though there's warmth in community, and disguise for the most part has been stripped away and we can see each other in desperate fellowship, the safe respite of home is crumbling away behind us as we go out from it.

"Can you see what I mean? My sons are gone to the rails, my daughters pine for them. My wife is with me only in some sausage in a greasy bag. And I am reduced to peddling a trap for animals."

→TWENTY-ONE←

Eastern State Penitentiary had been built over a hundred years before as a model for the future, both in design and attitude, that twisted Quaker idea in which solitary confinement and silence were means to proper meditation on one's crimes and failings, and thus rehabilitative. Constructed on the radial plan, the cell blocks were spokes running away from a central administrative hub, the steel door of each cell facing into a corridor and behind each cell a cloistered exercise yard. There were buildings between the spokes, most near the prison's exterior walls, a thick square of stone running thirty feet into the air and containing the entire eleven acres. When prisoners had entered these buildings they'd worn cloth hoods and were guided by guards as if they were blind men. Even the wheels of food and laundry carts were covered in leather casings, and the guards wore socks over their shoes as they moved silently through the cell blocks.

Now Eastern State was a mess of its original intentions, had fallen from them only a short time after its opening. Yet when I stepped from the taxicab and onto the pavement of Fairmount Avenue, I was impressed by the massive facade, those moss covered stone walls and the rectangular block of gothic offices at its impressive entrance.

It was seven at night and getting dark and I was exhausted, having slept little on the train. Still, I left my suitcase in the airless room and went out and walked the prison's perimeter in the failing light. My appointment with the warden was at three the next afternoon. I could bathe and sleep, have a late breakfast, refresh myself before that engagement. I wore the same clothing I'd worn on the train. I could feel grit at my shirt collar and the melting gum like thick sap under my wig. The hotel was small and rundown, a place for prison visitors I suspected, but I'd wanted to be close and Danker had arranged for that. It was good to get out of that room, to feel the cooling breeze that was coming on with dusk.

The hotel was directly across from the prison entrance. To either side of it were commercial establishments, a small grocery, a restaurant and a couple of shops. Then there were houses, those called trinities and a number of four-story ones, a church, and a few garages containing plumbing and automotive works. A row of houses faced into the prison wall on its west side, all under the shadow of that high stone. What an odd place to live, I thought, windows looking into the constant possibility of a fall from grace.

I wondered why the kid was here, why this place had been chosen. In the twenties, Eastern State had been designated as a maximum security prison, but this had become a joke in the profession. Just a few years before, during construction of a new spoke necessitated by an increase in population, no less than thirty escape tunnels had been discovered. And this was nothing new. The prison had been known as porous from the very beginning, and no change in administration had prevented escape. I walked under the shadows of its walls, thinking this over, curious about intentions. Then the sun was gone and the breeze grew stronger, though it was damp. I was ready for sleep. I went back to the room and raised the one window and pulled the thin curtains over it to block out the humidity. Then I removed the wig, showered and crawled between the sheets only in my skin.

The guard at the gate was expecting me. The gate was huge and could be opened fully to allow the entrance of vehicles. There was a smaller gate cut into it, and it was this one he opened and stood beside. Beyond him, through the high archway, I could see hazy figures moving in the bright sun and a shadowed figure, near where the archway ended, a boy no more than twenty years old I thought. He stepped tentatively forward as the gate clanked shut behind me. He wore a loose gray uniform and his hair was cut extremely short, his garments clean and recently pressed, and I could see his thin wrists at the cuffs. He didn't speak at first, just gestured with his hand, and I followed him, then moved up beside him as we went down a narrow stone hallway to the right.

"And why, exactly, are you here?" I asked, my voice low under the echo of our feet on stone.

"They called it malicious burning," he said. "It was a house for chickens, and it caught my fire's flames. They were country chickens."

"How long?"

"Two more years," he said, then added that he had been here for one.

We came to a stairway, wooden treads anchored into stone,

and when we reached the upper story, he gestured again, off to the left this time. In a few moments we were standing before a large wooden door, which he knocked upon, then opened immediately, stepping in and to the side to allow space for my entrance.

The warden sat at his desk, barred windows overlooking Fairmount Avenue behind him. The desk held papers and folders, all in neat order. The walls were hung with certificates and official-looking photographs, the warden beside various dignitaries in each of them. A row of statuettes, commemorative paperweights and mugs rested on a low bookcase along the west wall, positioned there with grave intention.

The warden was a tall man, dressed as I was, in seersucker, but his suit was light in color and speckled somewhat nattily. I thought he was checking the quality of my finely tailored one, his smile investigative as well as welcoming. His hair was grey and carefully combed and he wore a pencil-line mustache above his silk bow tie. He nodded and the boy turned and left the room. I heard the door close softly behind me. Then the warden was rising from his chair, coming out from behind the desk, his hand extended.

"Mr. Pollard," he said. "Let me welcome you."

He was pumping my hand and seemed unwilling to let it go. His grip was tight, but his arm flailed about above his wrist. He was slightly taller than I, and only when I asked him about the boy did he raise his eyes to my wig and release me from his grip.

"A trustee," he said. "Not a bad boy, really. He should be out by now. Parole? But there seems no possibility."

He gestured toward a leather chair before his desk, then moved back behind it as he spoke. We were both settled then in our respective places, his official, mine that of the interloper.

"Why?" I asked.

"The parole, you mean? It's this Depression. They need a promise of employment. Only then can they get out. And there are no promises these days."

"He's quite young," I said.

"Most are. Our average population has dipped in age from thirty-two to just over twenty in recent years. It's desperate thievery and things like that now. It's Depression. But we're getting ahead of the matter. How was your trip?"

"Fine," I said. "It was fine."

"Well," he said. "That's that. You know about our place?"

"A little," I said.

"And there's very little to tell. You can see it with your own eyes. We're maximum security, though that's not really important in these times. These young men, you know, they haven't a clue about escape."

"They took the kid near Scranton, I understand. Why do you think they sent him here?"

"I *know* why they sent him here. We're maximum security. He has somewhat of a reputation, don't you know."

"I know that," I said.

And I knew too of the porousness of this place and thought I was already getting some sense of the foolishness of its administration. Had they sent the kid here to avoid his escaping from a more respected prison? That seemed a possibility.

"Our only problem here is work," he said. "The unions. They've prevented any manufacturing. They say we're stealing jobs from free men who need them. That's perfectly reasonable, but what to do with our men? It's only exercise, gardening, a few noncommercial crafts now. Not a real problem. But the avoidance of boredom, you know?"

"I understand," I said. "But the kid, you have him chained and watched?"

"Oh, no!" he said. "Not anymore. That was when I wrote to you. We watch him of course. He's in solitary confinement, the only one here who is. He walks the yard now, in company of a guard of course."

"The laws?" I asked. "That chaining?"

"No, no, no, it wasn't that. He was pliable. Even somewhat pitiful. That was part of it. And we're maximum security you know. We're taking proper care with him now, but it seemed wrong and useless to keep him chained."

And what about me, I thought, then asked him that.

"Prudence," he said, "the wise thing," and his eyes jumped to the side briefly, avoiding my stare.

I knew then that the order for my consultation had come from somewhere above and was, as with the Arizona job, perfunctory. Just something for the record once the kid had managed his escape.

"If you could just give a few days study to this. Write up a report? That will be sufficient."

"I'd like to see him," I said. "Spend some time evaluating him. Then I can look over the physical plant."

"You do that? The human side?"

"Yes," I said. "I have."

"Well, okay. Why not. We can go there right now."

There were twelve-hundred prisoners in Eastern State and only nine-hundred and fifty cells. But the cells were quite large, designed for the prison's original intention, and could easily accommodate two and even three men, the older ones segregated from the youthful population.

"And we have the private exercise yards as well," the warden told me. "Really, there's plenty of room."

We'd gone down the stairway from his office floor, stepping out through a door into the prison proper, a V-shaped yard defined by two cell block spokes. He'd guided me along the outer wall until we were standing at the edge of a large garden, a plot of land in which the vines of tomato and bean plants were staked to upright sticks and rows of cabbage and lettuce were breaking through a rich, dark soil. A half-dozen boys were working in the garden, all in uniform and all with their hair cut short almost to baldness. They all looked like the kid, or what I remembered of him, subdued and contained, their clothing a kind of understated echo of their acceptance and resignation.

A few looked up at us, their eyes empty, yet somehow knowing, then looked the other way as a group of twenty or more came round at the far cell block edge flanked by two guards. They were going somewhere, not exactly in formation, but with clear intention, the guards at their perimeter herding them, and I could see that their similarity went beyond hair and the uniforms and was in their gait and expression, a look of dull and resolved comradeship.

"Just boys," the warden whispered at my shoulder.

But they were a strange tribe of boys, and it struck me that were they pushed to such extremity in other circumstances, not far from these, they might result in another kind of youth movement, one in which emblems and signs were sewn in over breasts and on the sleeves of their gray uniforms. They might have that cold, vacant look in their eyes still, but backed by a passionate intensity calling for the brutal action of revolution. Would the kid be king of this tribe then? He'd been that in other places. The group passed by, leaving a vacuum of cool stillness behind. I could feel it on my cheeks in the hot, humid air.

"It's the next one," the warden said.

In most of the cell blocks, the solid steel doors designed to keep prisoners solitary and in silence had been replaced with bars that allowed vision into the block's corridor, but in the one we entered they were still in place, slabs of impenetrable metal with narrow bins cut into them for the transport of food and other items. No light passed through the doors and the only illumination came from dim bulbs set in the high ceiling, though at the far end of the block, where it met the central administrative hub, sun flooded down from above. I could see figures moving through a sheen of dust motes there, growing more distinct as we moved along.

"These cells are for storage now, temporarily," the warden said. "He's down there, near the end."

I could see a steel door standing open in the distance, a wooden chair beside it.

"There?" I said. "Shouldn't someone be there?"

"Coffee, I suspect," the warden answered.

"But the door's open," I said. "He could walk out."

"Well, the doors are inhuman. And the only ways out are where we came in, which is locked now, and the hub, where there are always guards. But someone *should* be there. You're right about that."

We were close to the cell now. I could see a hard-edged shaft of light cutting across the passage floor, cast out from its interior. Then I touched the warden's sleeve.

"Look," I said. "I'd like to have him alone."

"Alone?" he said. "Good. That's fine. I can see about the guard. You can go on by yourself."

"And when you find him, could he move the chair away a little, give us some privacy?"

"That can be done," he said. "Whatever you need." Then he left me and strode down the passage toward the central hub.

The door was facing me, and when I stepped around it and looked into the cell, the kid's voice greeted me before I saw him.

"Good afternoon," he said.

Light leaked into the cell from above and through a doorway of mist in the distance, and as my eyes became accustomed to that moodiness, I saw the door itself, a gate opening into a garden. I could see a vine covered wall, moss growing between bricks, a few low planters spilling with vinca and variously colored petunias standing up from dark soil in them. I saw a stone fountain, then heard its soothing gurgling. A small thistle feeder hung from a wire, a goldfinch pecking for seed at its cylinder.

The kid sat on a wooden chair behind a small desk, a table lamp to his left, his cot against the wall across from him. I could see the chains and metal cuffs hanging from that wall and between the places of their anchoring, a large macramé hanging depicting a family of deer in some northern wood. All the walls of the cell were covered with pictures hung in a variety of hand-made frames, nature painting and photographs of animals, most of them dogs that looked very much like Young Lyle, who the kid knew only as Buck. A table sat off in the corner near the garden entrance, a hot plate and a tea kettle upon it, and on the wall above it, a narrow wooden shelf had been bolted in. I saw the row of tea tins and their exotic labels and a few leather-bound books.

"The library here is amazing," he said. "If one is amazed by such things. They've ten thousand volumes at least. Some of them are quite good."

He was rising from his chair, gesturing for me to enter. He wore the same uniform as the others, but his head was completely shaved, the blond cowlick gone. He looked much older now, though he was only twenty-two. I stepped into the cell, glancing up at the high barrel arch ceiling. There was a hole there at the center, perhaps a foot in diameter, the vertex of a cone of light, the base of which illuminated his desk and spilled over into angular fragments on the wooden floor, his carefully shined shoes stepping among them as he came to greet me.

"I'm afraid I've brought nothing for the housewarming," I said. He smiled into my eyes as he took my hand and shook it firmly.

"I understand. It's Mr. Pollard, isn't it?"

"You know that. Why don't you call me Chris. You once did."

"Naco," he said, and we both smiled in recognition of our common past.

He gestured toward the cot, apologizing for it, and once I was seated there, he went to fill the kettle at the spigot beside the toilet, then moved to the hot plate and put it up to boil.

"You have choices," he said. "Earl Gray, Darjeeling, many herbs, even chamomile. Isn't this the life?"

"I don't know," I said. "Is it?"

He took his chair again, then leaned back, tilting it until it pressed against the wall. I could see a discoloration above his forehead. Then he answered my question.

"I used to think so. I remember Pearce and Naco. That was only a year ago, and there was energy in it. But it feels more than just a year now, and I've grown sick of it. I've got all this and these many comrades too. Did you see them? They're my own age. We have everything in common and at the same time nothing in common. I don't know. You're looking at my scalp. It was an infection. They're very good about such things in here. One could get used to this."

It was not the blemishes I'd been gazing at, but the elegant shape of his bald head.

"Not like Louisiana," I said.

"Not quite. You were going there, weren't you?"

"I did," I said. "The place is finished. Did you know a man named Bonnefoy?"

"Of course," he said. "A good man. He made the place a little bearable."

"He's gone from there now."

"Is that so? These consultations of yours, they seem to be

bearing strange fruit."

"Indeed," I said. "But here we are. And I'm wondering why you haven't left this place. It's leaky. You could walk out anytime at all."

"That's right," he said. "And for the very last time. But I've been waiting for you."

As he'd been waiting at Pearce, I thought, where this had all begun. But I asked for no elaboration, nor did he offer any, for though both of us were sick of our professions now, we were still in them at that moment, and such articulations would have been unprofessional. In our opposing skills we were one thing, but that was not who we really were. I was of course fundamentally hidden, but I wasn't sure at all about him. His language and demeanor was what I remembered from that night in Naco, and his smile was the same too. Only a year ago, but now he seemed sad, even jaded, and I wondered if it was the prisons that had changed him, though I didn't think so. He seemed just a little depressed, though self-possessed and in complete control.

He poured the boiled water into a small, dark pot at the hot plate table, then lifted the pot and the two mugs and the strainer and returned to the desk. We waited while the tea seeped, then he poured it into the mugs and reached one of them across to me. We sipped at the hot brew. I heard the chair beyond the cell scrape against wood in the passage and assumed that the guard had come again and was moving it away for our privacy. The warden had not returned.

"He won't," the kid said. "He's busy with perambulations and meetings. He always seems to be."

"You know a good deal," I said.

"Well, this is home, a version of it anyway. They all were, but they seem to be disintegrating behind me. Like Louisiana now. Like what happened the first time."

"After your sister and the dog?"

"Buck," he said. "No. Before that. Even before Mr. Jones and my mother. When my father died? Each place has seemed a version of a home, all the various possibilities. Clear expectations, uncertainties, kindness, good fellowship and brutality, a safe room of one's own, as in this place. And permanence. But that's changing now. There's very little difference between the inside and the outside anymore. That's why it's over."

"And you have plans?"

"No. Not really. Do you?"

Fishing, I thought, and hunting, reading books and good eating, and wine, but it all seemed indulgence just then. Staying alive for a while. I thought I had plans for that.

In the prison of brutality and suicide they had beat him often and with cool detachment. "Whips and clubs, and sometimes with fists covered in leather, and with leather sleeves full of sand to hide the bruises, though there was no reason to hide them. They wanted me immobile and dispirited, and at times they accomplished that." And one time, for talking to others, they had beaten him senseless near the rack beyond the steel drawbridge, then carried him to a place he had no knowledge of and only gained a little once he came back into consciousness to find himself on the stone floor of a stone room, cushioned slightly in a bed of soiled straw that held the scent of human rot and those other ones, animal, and of the fields from which it had been cut and gathered. In the dark, and only a faint light at a deep, narrow window, a dungeon-like place at the castle's outer wall, yet not alone there, for he could see the eyes off in the shadows, but could not give spirit to the fear that they belonged to a rat or some other nocturnal beast.

"Jesse?"

The voice was rusty from misuse and without inflection and very old, he thought, and though they had beat the sides of his head, and his ears were swollen and ringing, and they had beat his eyes until they were closed up with fluid and grit from the hard ground they had forced his face into, he could hear him and even see him, though hazily, as he slipped slowly across the stone floor until he was sitting beside him.

"An old negro man, with a long wrinkled face, and I learned later that he had been there most of his adult life and was now near the end of it."

They had cast the kid there not for the company, but for the burden. To have him alone was no good and to have him among others he might well incite was no good either. The man was safe, too old for escape or the delivering of information to others, yet the kid would have to include his presence in any deliberations, drag him along in them, useless as he was.

"And I was Jesse. He knew the code of the name. Anyone who stood against them was Jesse. The body rendered into the leather container of the gone spirit out on the rack was Jesse. Almost everyone was Jesse, the name given to our common plight and any vestige of frustrated rebellion that might rise to change it.

"'Jesse,' he said, lifting my head up from the straw."

He heard the slosh of water in the bucket as it scraped on the stone floor, then felt the metal edge, lightly against his tender cheek and the flooding of water on his face and into his eyes and hair. He tried to open his eyes, but the grit was still there, and he only saw the shadow of the man's hand vaguely as he dipped it into the bucket, then heard the gargling and the spitting.

"I gots only this instrument," apologetic in a whisper, then he felt the fingers at his lids and the soft, probing tongue and heard the spitting of the grit, then the tongue once again, at the tear ducts to the sides of his nose now, and after that the familiar flooding of the water.

"We were at the stone wall then, and I was leaning against him. He had dragged me there, or I had helped in the dragging of myself. I don't know. But I smelled smoke. He was smoking something, the straw itself possibly, but a sweet scent. Then I felt his lips."

He was blowing smoke into the kid's ear for the soothing of it, warm there, and the rough lips, and the sweet scent in the kid's nose, and his breathing and whispering. Some song? But it was not that, just garbled grunts, and maybe a few words in the spaces between the breathing, the smoke washing across his ear and face as it drifted out again.

Then a cup at his lips, but not water. It was milk, something made from a stale powder, but milk nonetheless. I thought of Danker.

"That was home. A version at least. My father and my mother? Not really, for I was Jesse, and I gained a little heart then and had the wherewithal to continue on in recovery. And I was still Jesse when I escaped from there."

Someone had closed the heavy cell door, softly and with a quiet click only when the bolt slid to. I looked at the slab of metal, impenetrable.

"The shift changes," he said. "They get more careful as night comes on."

"Will it alter the plan?"

"Oh, no," he said. "That's part of it."

"They took you near Scranton," I said. "What got you there?"

Now it would be a year's story. He sipped at his tea, then set the mug down on the desk and leaned back in his chair.

Out of Pearce again. Then Naco and south into Cananea, rugged terrain and depression in another language, received more stoically there because of long experience, though the eyes were familiar, then up into Texas and through the panhandle, a sliver of Oklahoma, and into Kansas then and Wichita, where he found day work for a short time and joined in the soup and bread lines with all those others, many of whom had given up on escape. Then across another border and into Missouri and of two minds. He could go underground completely. Even at Pearce, prison was becoming the outside, the merging of two dire communities. Or he could find himself in yet another one, pushing again for that certain thrill, though it seemed gone now, or at least going.

Dusk came to the cell, and with it the cone of light shifted, its motes moving across the desk until his shoulders and face were in shadow and only his folded hands on the wood surface were in clear evidence. They were large hands, but his fingers were long and delicate, the nails cut straight across efficiently, and he was telling me of Saint Louis, where he had met a woman who was a beautiful woman, just twenty-one, who had lost her family to death and desperate travel and was alone, as he was, and on the move. Her hair was a fountain, her breasts small and invisible in his hands. They slept together under filthy blankets near a rail-head, but it was the stars he remembered, the same stars shining over the Rockefellers, and how they rose up in the cool morning, their bed lifted to become wrappings of warm clothing, and how they were as mobile as anyone. Maybe it was that, he said, and the fact that at Pearce there were those who were better off not being mobile. The tea had cooled in the mugs, the taste strong, a mix of pepper in berries like wine. They had parted near Terre Haute, and he had made his way northeast into Akron and politics, which was to become his "downfall. To name it dramatically," he said.

Light as feathers now in the cell, shadow fragments of vines and leaves from the garden cast piecemeal on the walls. They shimmered like winged figures, some animal, others human in miniature, boys and women with wings hovering in vibration, some perched on books and tea tins. I thought for a moment that he was rising, but he was talking of meetings and unions, a demonstration in front of some municipal building and that he had seen them looking, searching for particular faces in the crowd. Then he had left there and traveled by rail and foot across Pennsylvania and into depressed coal country. And something about Buck, his lost sister, but spring coming, and I ready to tell him or searching for the right time in the night now, the lamp unlit at the desk-edge, all feather figures gone, and a protest rally in front of some municipal building in the city of Scranton, where they had photographs and had followed him to his campsite, a dubious prize they took reluctantly. I was swimming, brushing her bobber, then I was climbing up to the rock ledge and Lyle and George Brankowski and his camera, and I was sitting beside Cora and Young Lyle, then was reaching back to get my wallet and the photograph, tilting, and he had risen and was bending over me and whispering, "you're a woman," then was slipping into the chair I'd made of myself for him, pressing back as if to enter and become me, my arms reaching to encircle nothing, the drug in the tea sweet in my nostrils, though bitter on my tongue. Then it was morning and there was sun in the cell, and I rose half-dreaming, costumed in the kid's prison uniform and his bald head and moved to the closed steel door and leaned heavily against it before starting in with the knocking.

They took me to an office in the central hub, where I was interrogated in the absence of the warden by a chief guard who had been apprised of my coming and the consultation. The warden would be gone and unreachable for the day. The guard was in charge of things and was taking his responsibility seriously, a simple holding action devoid of important decision powers. He was skeptical of everything I had to say.

I was bald and had no identification or civilian clothing, and though he knew I was not the kid and had put out the useless alarm, whistles and loud voices I could hear echoing through the cell block spokes, he doubted that I could be the consultant. He said we'd just have to wait for the warden's return the next day. He sat with his back to the sun so that it shone into my eyes, a crude and awkward move at best, and though I thought for a moment to reveal my woman's body, I knew that would only confuse the issue dramatically, and I kept myself hidden.

They put me back in the kid's cell, locking both the steel door and the heavy gate to the garden, and it was there I spent the day and night among the kid's belongings, passing the time in methodical searching. I looked behind the pictures and hangings, fingered through the pages of each book, and though I found things casually hidden, the drug vial tucked in the mattress ticking, a careful list of guard's names and schedules taped under the toilet's lip, I came upon only one thing that was truly private and went beyond the particular culture of that place in the kid's brief time there. It was a thin metal cylinder, a bullet cartridge no more than two inches long that was imbedded in a gouged out trough beneath the wooden shelf holding the books and tea. The trough had been cemented over with some gummy substance, stained with shoe polish to match the wood. It was a spent cartridge, and tucked down inside of it was a small rope of hair, three braids twisted together, which I carefully separated, then examined and smelled where sun entered the cell at the garden gate. I identified Young Lyle and the sweet scent of Cora. I suspected the other might be his mother's. There was no scent to it, but it was dark and oily and I realized it could even be mine, gone now into oblivion. Maybe it belonged to the woman whose hair was a fountain.

The next morning I was sitting in the warden's office again, and he was trying to gather me up in his agitated embarrassment.

"Of *course* I know it's you!" he said. "But how could he *do* this?"

He said the latter as if the kid had breached some social contract between them and he was offended.

"It's not the first time," I said. "He's very good at this. But it may be the last one."

"What do you mean?"

"I think he'll go underground this time. Change his identity. Things like that. I think it's over now."

"Well, it isn't for us!" he said, fighting for a clear resolve that in the following silence rung hollowly. I think he knew he'd been duped in the first place, by taking on the responsibility.

He said I could leave the clothing and the kid's shoes in the hotel room. They'd searched the place, and it was clear that someone had been there, but they thought nothing had been taken. They'd sealed it as a crime scene routinely, but I could break the tape and get my things.

"This has been one hell of a consultation," he said, his mustache twitching as he shook my hand.

"You can say that again," I answered, then turned and walked out through the door.

The kid had been in the room, though it was understandable that the warden's search had revealed nothing missing. He'd taken a pair of cotton slacks and a dark knit shirt and had folded the seersucker suit and packed it carefully under other clothing in the open suitcase. More significantly, when I looked through my wallet I found that the photograph was gone, the one George Brankowski had taken, Cora and Young Lyle and I on that day of fishing from the rock slabs. He had my shoes and wig as well, and I imagined he must look very much like me as he set out on his travels, going somewhere in disguise. His trick had been similar to the one used in that Oklahoma escape he'd described in Naco. Both involved costumes. I stood in front of the mirror, before removing his clothing. I didn't look like him at all, though of the same gender.

→TWENTY-TWO←

On a Monday early in August, Muffy appeared at the house stripped down elegantly for adventure. We'd be heading south, just two girls on a motor trip, stopping at small towns and old hotels, looking into shops and antique stores. Even traveling to see the Wisconsin Dells if we felt like it. The Duesenberg sat bright in the sun behind her as she strode across the parking area, dressed in slacks and a peasant blouse and a red beret to match her stylish tennis shoes. She skipped up the porch steps, then plopped down in a wicker chair across the table from me.

"Wow!" she said. "What a beautiful fucking day!"

"And free of all sweetness," I said. "Have they started yet?"

She'd closed Bo Peep's for a week of thorough cleaning.

Birds sang in the maze, but the house was perfectly quiet behind us.

"Yeah, yeah," she said. "First thing. There's chocolate everywhere and they'll have to use steam. I don't wanna see it!"

"Have a muffin," I said. They were on a plate on the table beside the pot. "And some tea."

Cora was off to Chicago with Virgo and Tallahassee, a last educational trip before school started. They'd be seeing the sights and museums, would spend the night in some hotel, then would return to the Southpaw house, where she and Young Lyle were staying while Muffy and I were on the road. Danker had left for fishing before dawn, and the Count and Bret had taken the week off for the same leisurely enterprise.

Since my return from Philadelphia, I'd put my efforts, which in this case meant my money too, where it would do the most good. I'd hosted a fundraiser at the house and had donated a significant amount to Phil La Follette's gubernatorial campaign. The Wisconsin Socialist Party had merged into the Progressive, urged by his rhetoric, a fact the Master Comrade took great pleasure in.

"On the map," he'd said. "We're moving toward the western sea. That's to the left, and Upton Sinclair."

"Another New Deal! Regurgence of the EPIC Plan!" Lyle had called out.

Still, at the grassroots, people were on the move or stationary in their poverty, untouched by the politics, and we both knew we'd be seeing evidence of that on our motor trip. I had an agenda for a few stops, at county jails and other small lockups, and would report back to La Follette's people. It would be anecdotal information, but of a very good kind in an election year. A few travelers were in residence on my land still, but not many. Summer was edging into fall, and most had pulled up stakes and headed south.

"What do you hear from Hans?" Muffy said. "And Avery?"

"They've moved into the old man's house in Minneapolis. I gather they're still working toward a settlement of some kind. It's mysterious."

"I don't fucking think so," Muffy said.

"Is it only 'fucking' today?"

"Shit, no. It's early! What about your papers? Isn't that Minneapolis too?"

I'd spoken to Danker, then filed for the adoption where I still had the power of my father's influence. Cora had no discernible sources, but for the ones I'd learned of in the kid's stories in Naco. That might have been cause for a thorough and dragged out search, but I seemed to be getting around that now, having kept silent about my uncertain knowledge. The house and farm could be there still, and available to her, but I'd decided to let that rest, at least until the adoption became final.

Danker had agreed, both to the adoption and the silence.

"Well," he'd said. "A new kind of family, and who am I?"

"The father," I said. "Who else?"

It was while the troupe was packing up to leave that Cora came to her decision. I was in a blue funk, sitting on the porch in robe and slippers, hearing Blondie's whinny and the sounds of voices speaking in activity from the rear of the house. The Master Comrade sat across the table from me, sipping coffee. I'd spoken to George, Lyle and the Darlings, all but Cora, who had avoided me.

"Well, it's this way," the MC said. "She doesn't want to be leaving. She wants to stay here. So does Young Lyle."

"How can you know that?" I said.

"It's human-animal logic. Where she goes, he goes."

"I didn't mean that," I said. "How can you be sure of her? That she's sure?"

"That's not it," he answered. "If it were, it would be you

and not her. But nothing is sure. In life, I mean. You have to make it up as you go along."

"Following your heart?" I said. "That's not like you."

He laughed. "The polyterritans again? Those values? No, I wouldn't say that. It's been the cause of great troubles historically. It needs backing with clear reason of course and didn't often have that. The heart can be a terrible fascist, or the cause of one. But in this case?"

"Can you bring her around?" I said. "She's been avoiding me."

"Of course she has," he said. Then he lifted his hand and snapped his fingers, and when I turned to the side I saw George Brankowski standing in the doorway smiling. He opened his palm and a mockingbird appeared on it. Then it squatted and flew off into the day, and Cora stepped out from behind him, dressed for travel in a plaid skirt and blouse from my childhood, her eyes bright and misty under my sailor's cap. She'd slimmed down in her time at the house and seemed taller than when I had first met her, not a young woman yet, but getting there, no longer just a child coming out of a baby.

"Come over here," I said.

And she did. She took the Master Comrade's seat, and he and George withdrew into the house for our privacy. Her feet touched the floor now, and she sat with her hands in repose, looking across the table.

"Would you like to stay here with me?" I asked.

She shifted her hips on the chair, eyes blinking, as if she were considering the offer.

"And with Danker? And with Virgo and Tallahassee? Young Lyle too?"

"That comes with the deal."

She didn't hesitate then.

"Yes," she said.

"But are you too old to sit on my lap?"

"Not yet!"

She said it brightly and with a smile.

"Well, okay," I said. "Come over here then."

And that was it. And there were no tears or spoken promises. Lyle and Cora took a moment together in which they hugged each other at the door of the battered truck, and Lyle tossed the ball to Young Lyle one last time.

"Commemorates logic of the dryalectic!" he called out, and Young Lyle barked in agreement.

The Darlings and George Brankowski hugged both of us, and the Master Comrade squatted down until he was the same size as Cora and spoke to her in quiet detail of private things. Then he rose to his feet somewhat stiffly and moved to where I was standing and pressed his head against my chest.

"I hear it," he said. "Even better without breasts."

And then they were gone.

"I'm raring to go, Chris," Muffy said. "Are you ready?"

"You bet," I said. "I'll get my satchel."

"And I'll put the Dues's top down," she said, jumping up quickly from her seat.

The house was locked up tight, all but the front door, and I could see the immaculate shine on everything, even the statue of Helios, as I climbed quickly up the curving staircase and went to my bedroom. I had the satchel in my hand, but I set it down again and went back to the hallway and moved to Cora's new room for a quick look.

George Brankowski had cleaned it, as he had everything else in the house, but it was Cora herself who had seen to the organization. Pictures hung on the wall, her clothes carefully in the closet.

She'd searched out objects from my childhood, ceramic pots and wooden souvenirs, and had placed them on shelves and furniture in a private order, making them her own. In that moment, I felt I had the chance to live it all over again, in the life of another, but I threw that away. Such ideas were in the past now, and I was finished with masquerade.

I wore a pair of loose gabardines and one of my father's fine silk shirts that I'd belted tight at the waist with links of Mexican silver. I'd tucked an old straw hat over my bald head for the sun. Muffy drove like a demon, and I'd have to take it off once we were on our way. I wore new canvas deck shoes and was sure-footed as I stepped quickly down the stairs.

Muffy had pulled the Duesenberg close up to the porch steps and she revved the powerful engine when she saw me at the door. The formal garden was bright in the sun beyond her, and the juniper tips drifted in a light breeze above the maze, its archway entrance like some empty niche awaiting a statue.

I had the hair of the kid's sister and of his dog, and their sentient bodies too. He had the photograph and his abilities.

One of these days, I thought. He'll be standing right there.